THE SCIENTIST

A Short Essay and Two Stories

THE SCIENTIST

A Short Essay and Two Stories

Alex Pucci

authorHOUSE®

AuthorHouse™
1663 Liberty Drive
Bloomington, IN 47403
www.authorhouse.com
Phone: 1-800-839-8640

Published by AuthorHouse   09/07/2012

ISBN: 978-1-4772-6430-0 (sc)
ISBN: 978-1-4772-6429-4 (e)

Library of Congress Control Number: 2012915976

To Gino

ESSAY

"Is there a *Homo Scientificus*?" My son asks me.

I can't say there is. We are all distinctive and different, both in the way we think and in the way we do our work. Of course scientists have in common specialist training and follow certain rules. Not unlike philosophers, they have adopted a precise way of reasoning.

Yet it's necessary to qualify scientists by their own times: in 200 BC, Greek scientist Archimedes didn't have many scientific rules to follow. In fact, he was the one who discovered some of nature's rules for bodies displacing water when plunged into it. Eighteen centuries later, Galileo and Kepler still strived to find basic rules for the physical universe, rules that took a long time to be accepted as scientific.

For his part, Leonardo da Vinci considered himself an artist, although the many inventions he made were the result of high technological skill. But in his days technology was synonymous with art. In those times, during the Renaissance, scientific knowledge was limited: a good "scientist" would probably know all there was to be known. Nowadays a scientist is hard-pressed to know it all just in his own specialty.

Experiment and empirical proof are words that may well define scientists. Their job is to find the proof of a theory (or to try to disprove it). But time, once again, is the key. Current experimental methods are elegant examples of how testing has evolved with time. In the 19th Century, when Pasteur and Koch first developed the germ theory of disease, scientists didn't hesitate to inject themselves with scab and pus to prove they could become immune to particular germ infections. And they did. Today very large scientific teams use immense machines like the Large Hadron Collider to prove that certain subatomic particles exist.

The character of a scientist then imputes creative distancing from the past, both in theory and in experiment. In the period of the Enlightenment, from the 17th Century onwards, this rapture from the past involved greater reliance on reason rather than faith. Voltaire, taking his cue from Francis Bacon, thus became the standard-bearer of the movement that was to revolutionize science. Chambers' and Diderot's Encyclopedias put on paper all that was known at the time, thus giving scientists a wide base on which to step up, launch further theories and accelerate knowledge.

This was a time of great advances in physics and Newton was at the very center of it: his theory of universal gravitation and his laws of motion changed the scientists' view of the world, and provided explanations for physical events on earth and earth's place in the universe.

Space was then an impossibly distant domain that scientists later conquered with the advent of radio. Marconi's experiment in December 1901, with the transmission of a message across the Atlantic Ocean, showed that it was possible to communicate far and fast on radio waves. Today the largest radio telescope, the SKA, is at the early stages of construction, but once built it will open up exploration to the farthest galaxy.

In life sciences biology needed physics for the experiment that Galvani used in the 1780s when he applied an electrical current to severed frogs' legs. It gave rise to a new generation of scientists who would reflect and work on this mix: if we can contract muscles with electricity, is electricity carried also by nerves? Is electricity an element of the action that goes on in the brain?

Scientists had to change their biochemical view of the body to the idea that electricity, as well as chemistry and biology were closely linked there. But it was only in the second half of the 20ᵗʰ century that Andrew Huxley found the experimental way to show how in the brain the three disciplines joined together for neuron firing.

Those scientists had to wrestle with an ever-changing view of the world, one that was in a state of rapid evolution. Both life scientists and physicists worked and theorized increasingly without being able—in their own lifetime—to prove by experiment what they had put down in theory. That is what Einstein did by relying on mathematics to devise elegant formulas that could explain his theory of relativity in the organization of space and time. Proof came about in subsequent generations and the value of scientists like Einstein grew all the more.

Nowadays we marvel at the ability of Peter Higgs and colleagues to predict in 1964 the existence of a subatomic particle that would complete the theoretical "Standard Model" of the atom in physics. Forty-eight years later, the Higgs Boson particle has finally been detected in a colossal experiment that involved many hundreds of scientists and some 27 kilometers long equipment. The character of the scientist has changed fundamentally with the decoupling of those who devised the theory from the many more who proved it.

In life sciences this is the case in a few other instances: in the first half of the 19ᵗʰ century, Darwin's account of evolution didn't really explain the fundamental mechanism of this natural phenomenon. Later in that century the monk Mendel, in his much smaller exploration of the genetics of peas, found the very substrate—inherited traits—on which evolution could operate. Much later, in the 20ᵗʰ century, Crick and Watson studied the molecular structure of genetic DNA and found the mechanism, which explained how it was capable of passing on the coded information that characterizes a living species. When this genetic copying changed by chance (mutation), the evolution of the species could take flight.

In life sciences, scientists had to split themselves more thinly and quickly came to adopt new sub-disciplines. In my lifetime, for example,

I have seen the surging of molecular biology as a separate field: it didn't exist as such during my postgraduate studies.

The contemporary life scientists have had to split, but at the same they had to be capable of assembling systems like genomics: the science that studies the full complement of our genes as a whole. And, while the splitting of research fields—say, becoming a molecular geneticist—would in a sense "purify" the topic, it wouldn't be enough unless he "congregated" with other disciplines like bio-informatics in order to study the system of genomics. These yo-yo movements—between the molecular level on one hand and system biology on the other—characterize modern life scientists. In a similar way scientists who work today in particle physics at the subatomic, infinitesimal scale would have to assess the significance of their work in the realm of astrophysics, namely in the immensity of the universe.

The splitting of the atom brings our minds back to the 1940s, when the dual use of nuclear power to create energy and bombs became a dark reality. Then the conscience of scientists and their subjectivity became more prominent in the clean-cut world of science.

So, time and space, scale and specialties, conscience and ethical dilemmas characterize scientists in different ways and make the search for a common *Homo Scientificus* very difficult. Perhaps the only characteristic we have in common is the drive to know and discover new rules of nature: in other words, our curiosity and passion for science.

In the two stories that follow, this drive is clear but it is applied to different ends. Passion for science leads the protagonist of the first story to invest herself in "ferrying science across to the wider world", to communicate its results and to see that the acquired knowledge is of benefit to the world at large. Her attempts are persistent and her drive unabated even after some failures.

In the second story, passion for science shows its negative side in blinding the protagonist to reality and ethical rules. Scientific arrogance takes over, while her lack of resilience shows up and leads to trouble.

The narrator of both stories is a scientist himself, but one with a more absolute drive: to find the truth. In science, he knows, one can only achieve an increasing approximation to the truth, so his quest is unending.

The two scientific stories also raise some ethical dilemmas: the first one deals with the value of scientific discovery against "brigands" who will not understand it. The second raises the issue of what power scientists should have over a potential improvement on biological normality. Of course scientists are human and both stories deal with the recurrent matters of life: love, marriage, vanity and ambition, anger and powerlessness.

And, since we are talking of scientists who know how Emotion can influence Reason, why not add a touch of metaphysics with Janet Laurence's images? She takes us beyond ordinary visual perception into a space where our memories interact with her artwork in mysterious ways. I think even Voltaire would have approved.

Alex Pucci
Sydney 23.8.2012

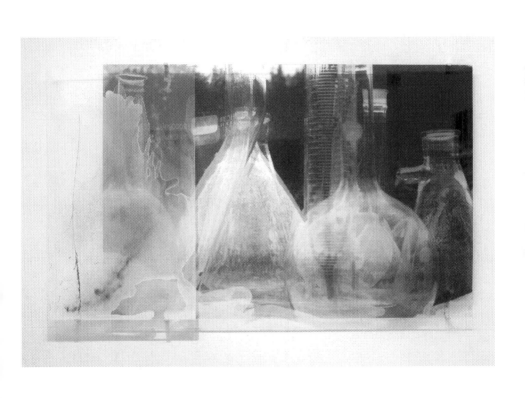

Memory in Glass (detail 1)

Memory in Glass (detail 2)

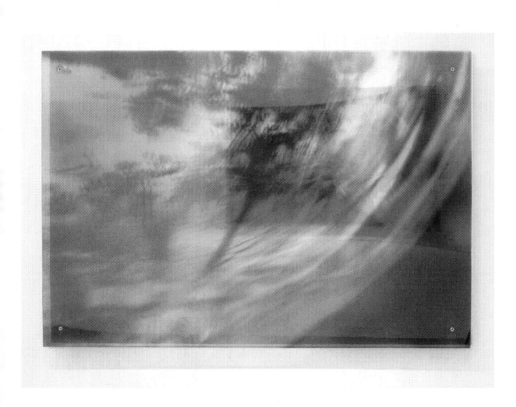

Memory in Glass (detail 3)

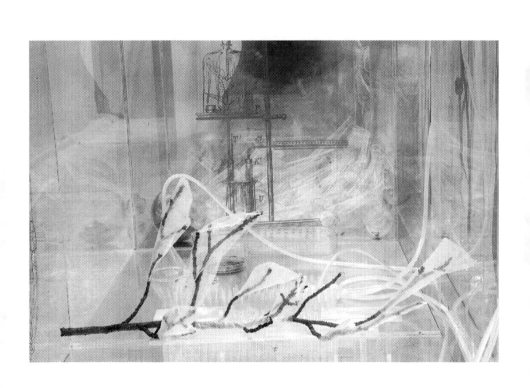

Waiting

Bourse Brigands

The vessel of the soul lies not
in the heart but in the brain
Leonardo da Vinci

One

14 December 2014. "Did you say number 26?" the driver asks.

"Yes, it's the house on the corner, the one with a sandstone wall."

The black car stops across my driveway. I'm home. A silent, shut home, but that's fine. As soon as the car is gone, I start walking towards the gate but stop and touch a stone block of the wall that is closest to the steps leading up to the house. I search a particular sign and find it quickly: 4, carved at that age with a toy spanner as soon as I had learnt how to write numbers. It's a secret mark that is now almost invisible. Time, wind and dirt have managed to cover up its groove but for me, touching it is a little and necessary ritual when I come back home from afar.

Steps up, landing, more steps to the right and I'm on the upper deck of my ship, overlooking the corner that for me is the bow. The lower deck has lawn and pool but I aim beyond that and look over towards the small cove of Edwards Bay. Welcome back.

My bags touch the polished boards of the timber floor and make a creak as I rush to the mail tray on a table in the hall. A letter; how unusual these days. It's an old-style envelope with airmail stripes all around it, rudimentary paper and a post stamp I don't recognise. There is no sender's name on the back. I open it quickly and turn the pages to the bottom; it's signed 'Alba'.

Mio Caro Amico

You are still my dear friend, even after a silence of sixteen years. Because time does many things to us: it forms deep wrinkles on our faces but also fine embroidery on our minds. So time can trick us to believe that it was dormant, unmovable until we link up again after a long pause.

This is it, our reunion breaking my silence with a piece of good news: your work on olfactory neurons has helped me to develop a quick test that detects mental damage in children who have gone through trauma of war or famine.

You'd have noticed from my envelope that I am in Africa—Eritrea to be exact—a country that has had, more than most, long and violent clashes. Many children were involved, some suffered trauma but others did not. It was this difference that intrigued me and pushed me to apply your study on olfactory neurons. I wanted to know if it was suitable to distinguish those who have from those who have not suffered mental trauma.

Well, we made it. We have been able to devise a new biological test that can single out those traumatised children who need particular, urgent care. And you were at the origin of all this. So, in writing a paper that will be published next month on "Reviews of Medical Diagnostics", we have given due recognition to your work. You'll see it if you look it up on the net.

Of course this will bring back to mind the dreadful period of our encounter with the fraudsters, our Bourse Brigands. A time charged with complications of more than one kind, of memories you probably wish to have deleted.

Nevertheless, I expect you to be glad, perhaps vindicated and able to change the measure of your work in more positive terms. I've done that and on this note must plunge back into my silence.

You know ALBA

The Scientist

I find myself in the street at the top of the steps leading to The Esplanade: rush down, cross the small park, walk on the sand and start kicking the waves. Kicking with rage, over and over. I notice people looking surprised, shaking their heads, moving further away.

"Just angry," I say, "not dangerous!" and start walking along the beach, feet still kicking occasionally. Yes, angry with her. She just cuts, as always, cuts across all normal expectations, cuts me out and then cuts loose. She did it in '98, she's done it now. And I sit here on the humid sands trying to make sense of it. Why this much rage? My memories of that time are not easily accessible, as if packed in a tight ball. OK, I could move around it in the periphery and try to find an opening, a thread to pull them out. And then? How would I cope with the rush?

*

When I get back home, Martina's car is in the driveway. She told me on the phone that she'd be in Palm Beach for a wedding and stay overnight at Bonnie's, a close friend. Stepping up to the first landing, I take the path to the left and around the house to the back. I knock at the kitchen door and Martina opens straight away:

"I was wondering where you were." She kisses me lightly, our mouths touching briefly.

"On a walk along the beach. You look well." It's true.

"Some breakfast?" she offers, as if my compliment needed a payback. "Fruit, nuts and yoghurt?"

"Yes, please! I'll have a quick shower."

Martina's presence is calming. She has the refreshing habit of making you think of practicalities—pleasant ones.

"Do change into something smart." She follows me as I run upstairs. "We are going somewhere."

"Where?" I stop and lean over the rail.

"Shopping for a cake first, then to my mother's for a family reunion." She smiles.

"Any particular occasion?"

"Your son's birthday." She stops but doesn't leave it at that: "I'm sure you got a present for Max in Paris."

"And you are right, as always."

*

The breakfast table on the veranda is set immaculately, the glass top over timber reflecting containers with coffee and milk, pastries and fruit juice plus my long glass carefully striped by layers of fruit, yoghurt and nuts. Martina has put out our yellow-and-white-muslin place covers with assorted napkins.

"Nice touch," I say.

She smiles again while pouring the coffee and asks in a friendly voice:

"Do you want to talk about the letter? I found it spread out on this table; I'm afraid I couldn't help it and read it. Good news, isn't it?"

She sounds sincere but I'm not sure what to say; there are too many things in that letter.

"I mean the test," she continues. "Your work has ended up being put to such good use! I'm thrilled about that."

"Of course, it's great. It was certainly not planned that way, still I'm glad." I sound flat, controlled, and unable to hide anything from Martina.

"I knew about your affair with Alba," she says after a pause.

"But you didn't say anything at the time! Why?" I'm amazed.

"Would you have wanted me to? Would it have changed anything?"

"Probably not, but you had the right to discuss it, at the very least."

"Well," she says with a look of regret, "that's exactly what I didn't want to do. I was afraid you'd leave. And you were in such a state of confusion . . . ."

"Was I?" I look at her as to some source of truth.

"Yes, especially when she left. I don't know how you remember it but you were sort of stunned."

"Well, I'm sorry about that." I feel embarrassed.

"Don't worry. At the time I couldn't do anything else to keep you."

I find her matter-of-factness unsettling. My mind goes back to her revelation—she knew!—that keeps shaking my memories. I start seeing our marriage as a quiet lake where, all of a sudden, proof after proof emerge like bubbles of air, pointing all to one conclusion: Martina's approach, ever professional, understanding and practical, made of her part in our marriage a job well done but now it seems to me just a job. And I begin to regret my attitude in our life together, that of being an open book in front of her superficial reading:

"You seem quite blasé about it. I wish I could do the same."

"Why don't you write something up on that period? Not necessarily about the affair but on the events Alba mentions in the letter. It should do you good. You've always said you find writing therapeutic."

"Yes, perhaps that's something I should do."

"And now let's talk about something cheerful."

She launches into a detailed account of the Palm Beach wedding and turns suddenly into a witty social reporter. The second marriage of our friend Kelvin, after twenty-five years in the first, must have attracted some quirky people.

An engineer/inventor, Kelvin apparently asked some colleagues to show their skills and imagination on their partners' attire. One came up with a sort of hydraulic shoe heels that his wife could vary depending on the person in front of her, or on her state of tiredness. Another lady came in the afternoon sun with a large-brim hat that retracted like a folding door, shrinking its size towards sunset. The most stunning was apparently a tight dress printed like a perfect nude, an incredibly realistic replica of a beautiful woman's body. But she was too distracting and had to change her dress before the ceremony.

While Martina talks, I think of our marriage: why didn't she leave me then? I can't remember her being that attached to me. Was it convenience? Love has a sedate quality these days and possession of the other doesn't come into it. I can't remember it being different sixteen years ago, so why did she stay with me? If there was anything else between us, I can't remember, nor do I remember if things changed in Martina at that time. Perhaps we were already so distant from each other that when Alba came on the scene there was no need to push Martina aside. She remained at her place.

Giggles interrupt Martina's story several times, uncontrollably. I try to join in the laughter, not an easy thing while I'm eating.

"Well," she gets up at the end of her story telling, "we'll need to go there early and help Mum to prepare lunch, but also perhaps you'd want to talk with Max? And do you think you'll be able to rescue your playful soul?"

***

Two

31 March 1996. His photo on the Institute newsletter reminds me of why I'm here. It's Professor Boyle, our chief. I wasn't one of his students, as is often the case; I joined his group later, having already gained my stripes overseas in continental Europe. I returned to Australia thanks to a government scheme of five-year Fellowships, a sort of reverse brain-drain measure that provided security and good conditions. I could have taken my Fellowship anywhere in Australia but I chose him. Why?

I like Professor Boyle. He is gentle without being a pushover and quite interested in the work of our lab, where he says he'd like to return one day. But his big resource is political skill. Staff politics, the boardroom, funding, government—all areas are within his smooth reach. Unusual for a scientist who made important discoveries in molecular biology while working in the US. He came back to Australia to head our Medical Research Institute that bears his name. The building is brand new, ten floors of laboratories and offices surrounding an atrium that opens all the way to the top and spreads natural light everywhere inside.

In the middle of the atrium an open staircase in the shape of a helix is used more often than the lifts, since our movements are usually up or down only a couple of levels. Today I came up from the 7th to the 9th floor, the Prof.'s. He's summoned me for a meeting at 10.30 but of course he's a bit late. I sit on one of the armchairs clustered around the atrium and re-read the memo he sent me a couple of days ago.

CONFIDENTIAL

We need to discuss an opportunity for funding a side project in your lab. I have received an offer to participate in a joint venture with a prospective Biotech company to be headed by Dr Alba Gruber—if her share issue is successful. As you may know, I am trying very hard to attract funds to the Institute beyond government grants and Fellowships like yours.

Melbourne has had of course a head start for its institutes with donations from "old money" over the past three or four decades. It also had the luck of two Nobel Prizes, which have attracted international brains. Sydney is not in their league, despite pockets of excellence. The wealth of Sydney is less stable but entrepreneurial and the Biotech industry here is more mature and sophisticated than in Melbourne. This is what we need to tap into.

Dr Gruber is a pioneer in Biotech: this new entity, if successful, would be her third. I am impressed by the business model she is proposing. It makes sense and is equitable for all participants. The Boyle Institute is one of four her company intends to fund. I do not know at this stage anything about the others but in our case she has expressly selected your neuroscience lab. I would nominate you as project leader if you accept.

Let's talk. Denyse will call you to arrange a time.

I didn't like the idea when I first read it. I don't like it now. It seems disruptive, at least distracting. My well-planned project, funded by a five-year Fellowship, is only in its second year but is on schedule. It's great not to have to write grant applications for a while; it feels good to concentrate, to know exactly what my assistants and my Ph.D. students demand of my time.

We've agreed on every step: on the conferences we'll be going to, on the papers we'll write, on the posters we'll construct. It was all sketched out—and now this. If it's a Biotech project, it means it will have industry restrictions, secrecy requirements and the rest. Am I going to build Chinese walls in the lab?

And the reporting? How many hours would I need to spend on the Biotech project for their money? I can only spend 20% of my time in extra Fellowship activities. No, it doesn't square at all.

"James." Denyse is suddenly in front of me. "Rob will see you now."

How powerful does she feel in calling me by my formal name while using the abbreviation for HIM? I follow her.

"Jim, come in." Professor Boyle is sitting not at his desk but at the round table in his office that is used normally for small meetings with senior staff. "All is well?" He remains seated, a position that has some advantage given his shorter size.

"It was perfect, until I got your memo." He likes frankness; he's got it. But my tone is friendly.

"I see," he says, looking at me in the eyes for a split second, before turning to Denyse: "Could we have coffee and no interruptions? Ok, you know, Jim, I had exactly the same reaction when Alba approached me."

"Alba? Do you know her personally?"

"Oh yes, we've been on the same government advisory Council for Biotech since 1993, I think."

"And what's she like?" I saw her photo in the press a few years ago.

"An original mind in an attractive shell. She has a peculiar personality but is passionate about Biotech and extremely sensitive to ideas that push the boundaries of science."

"I've read she's got science and also business backgrounds." I find the mix quite exotic.

"Yes, she did an MBA at our Uni, in the Graduate School of Management." Denyse brings the coffee and he starts sipping it straight away, hot as it is. "I knew you'd find the whole thing disruptive, but she insisted on your lab. We'll probably miss out if you won't take it." He appears a little tired now, or resigned.

"Why my lab?" I'd like to know anyway.

"She's obviously interested in neuroscience and read your recent paper on the potential for neurogenesis in olfactory neurons."

"But how could you possibly consider accepting her proposal? Have you thought it through?" I like to challenge him as he's usually a good sport.

"Yes, I have actually. The agreement with her company would provide for about two million dollars over three years on a project of your choice, subject to their agreement. This would cover the purchase of the confocal microscope you've been asking for, plus salary and consumables for four research assistants. They would take on all the bench work, writing up data and results. In fact, in their free time they could help you in your own experiments."

"And my role?"

"To plan the R&D and supervise your assistants, plus write up reports and participate in management meetings." He speaks mechanically with seemingly little interest.

"What do you mean, management meetings?"

"Alba has devised a new management system she wants to try in this venture: all project leaders—there would be four of you—would meet every month to discuss and vet one project per meeting. So each project would come up for discussion every four months." He looks at his watch and seems keen to end our conversation. "Really," he says, "there is no point in spending more time on this, given your objections."

"Well, do you want me to think it over?" I offer.

"It would be great if you did. It's a substantial sum for research, but also I think it could serve as a spearhead, a forerunner for more projects like this, if it works." He looks at me carefully; he hasn't won yet.

"Ok, I'll think about it if you guarantee it won't lead to longer hours."

"You have my word, so we'll avoid your wife exercising her legal expertise if I am wrong on this." He stretches a wry smile as I go and lets me out.

I leave with an unpleasant feeling that seems lodged at the back of my throat. Why? I need to know: no brooding though. Let's play. It's a quick game I play in my mind to deal with a subconscious impression that bothers me. I turn a conversation into a ball game—basket this time—where two players bounce and pass a ball that changes character with the sense of the exchange.

Rob and I are in the frontcourt, facing each other with a smile. He's got the ball, bounces it and passes it to me; it has the color of authority—it's light and direct. I catch it and bounce it forcibly, impressing a charge that becomes despondency, then throw it with a wide, curving cut. Rob receives and bounces the ball delicately, as if trying to discharge it, then passes to me the color of patience—or is it a trap? I respond by moving to the backcourt while bouncing and then pass to him my curiosity. He stays the course, calmly, and throws at me substance and facts. The ball I receive is heavy now, but those facts have ME written all over and I respond instinctively with a cast of self-importance. Now Rob moves quickly, playing a ball fake with a sudden bounce that causes me to move in the wrong direction while he turns back, dribbling rapidly towards the backboard. And it is here that I see the color of my vanity going through the net. Rob has scored.

***

Three

15 April 1996. Of course I gave in, but it wasn't a backflip because my earlier bout of myopia was easy to correct. At first I hadn't seen the same picture as our prof. He treats some problems as small parasites rather than large hurdles. Well, my parochialism was clearly one of those small bugs that I was able to brush off and out of my way. No need to linger on that.

As I drive home in the early evening, I recall with a certain pride how quickly I adjusted to the events. In only two weeks I've made all the preparations: turned my mind to search and design a new three-year project, wrote it up, discussed it with Rob, changed a few things and finalised it. All within the time allowed by the Fellowship.

Then I prepared the lab staff for this important visit. My speech to the young people who work in my lab was perhaps reminiscent of Rob's words, I admit it, but what's wrong with that? They seemed convinced, perhaps for different reasons. I don't mind. Was it the fact that our new research assistants would push our numbers up to ten, more than the nine in the 'Bone and Metabolism' lab? Or the fact that we'd be in charge of the confocal microscope that everyone else would want to use? It doesn't matter; they are happy and so am I.

This morning at eleven, Dr Alba Gruber paid us a visit. She came along with Rob, listening to him attentively as they entered my lab. Nothing formidable about her from a distance: dressed in a suit of neutral colours, moderate square heels and medium length brown hair. She looked unremarkable.

"Alba, here is our Dr James Corsini." Rob makes the introduction half-facetiously. The other part of his tone betrays a sense of relief for getting to this point.

"Welcome to our lab, Dr Gruber." I shake the hand she is offering and feel a strong and unusually warm touch.

"I am grateful for the privilege, Dr Corsini." Her accent sounds slightly foreign.

Again Rob grabs her attention: "Come, Alba, and meet the staff." He goes through the usual protocol as he moves with her along the benches where people sit on stools, or past the cubicles where they work at their desks. Some, in front of a particular piece of equipment, are asked to explain what they are doing. I follow. From up close her jacket reveals a very interesting pattern: small checks alternating dark green and off-white, both with specks of several colours—yellow and brown, light blue and brilliant green. The skirt, with the same basic material but a different pattern, gives away the exclusivity of the well-cut suit, one of the tricks my mother used to decide on the elegance of other women.

"Jim, would you like to show Dr Gruber some of your work? I'll see you both in my office when you're finished. We have to talk about the project." Rob leaves at that stage and I take over.

We go next door in a small seminar room where I have prepared a slide show.

"I've put together for you some images of olfactory neurons and their surrounding tissue in the bulb." I know this is the starting point of our project.

She sits at one side of a narrow table where the projector is ready to be lit up and I stand on the other side.

"Yes, I've seen some of your work on paper, where the images were only in black and white." She takes a file out of her bag, opens it and reveals my article with a number of question marks on the margins. "So I have a few questions that perhaps you'll answer in your presentation." Again a foreign accent creeps up, not an obvious one.

"May I see what you are referring to?" I approach her across the table and perhaps startle her. From up close I look at her extraordinarily soft face but her eyes give me a definitive stop. Dark brown with pupils restricted by the proximity, they seem so deep that vertigo comes to mind. I look at my paper on the table and retreat.

"Yes, I have the very same images in colour, and from the staining of the different markers, you'll see exactly what they mean." I turn on the projector.

"The first slide is a 10x40 times magnification of an olfactory epithelium biopsy: in brown you'll see olfactory neurons stained by a marker protein that identifies mature neurons."

"How do you identify mature from growing cells?"

"Here it is. This slide shows neuronal precursor cells labelled with p75NGR antibody. The next one shows a further stage of maturation with cells stained by GAP43: they are growing but are still immature neurons."

"Why do you show the various stages of maturation? What's the significance?"

"Because neurons in the olfactory bulb have the unique characteristic of growing anew, even in mature people. I mean they continue to regenerate and are unique in that they grow continuously throughout life."

"So that they would show the effects of disease and trauma in their growing pattern." Alba seems very happy about this.

"Exactly." I'm impressed by her quick mind.

"Do you want to show me more slides?"

"Yes, of course; perhaps you want to see evidence of our lab's techniques?"

"I'd like to see how you go about taking biopsies to extract the neurons."

"Here is the procedure to take nasal biopsies under local anesthesia."

"It all seems very straightforward. And is it safe?" Alba asks while taking some notes on numbers and size of the biopsies.

"The next slides, very quickly, show how many we've done with no damage to the patients."

"The nasal biopsy, does it have alternatives?"

"No, not really. It provides information on the structure and maturation of neurons as no other method can, save an autopsy."

"So through the olfactory bulb, you get as close as you can to the central nervous system, short of digging a hole in the head!"

She seems more relaxed now and smiles at last. Perfect teeth, of course. I didn't expect anything else, but I wish I could find her at fault somewhere. Rob said 'a peculiar personality'. What did he mean by that?

"Then I take it that you have worked out a technique to draw samples from the olfactory bulb that can be used to analyse the presence and maturity of growing neurons and their possible changes in disease and trauma." Alba says this with her chin slightly raised.

"That's right. Now have a look at this; it's my best image."

On the large screen, bright neurons dominate the field with their green/violet colours, yet the yellow fibers that stem from them and connect neurons to many others seem the site of real action.

Alba is captivated. "Neurons that fire together, work together! I remember this."

"I know."

She has gone under the colourful image of neuron connections to the level where chemical signals open up molecular gates and activate a rush of electric ions that will travel along the fibers in many directions all at the same time, creating an excitation that is powerful because it is collegial. In that microscopic, firing world we meet: not in the superficial image with its artful colours, but in the underlying complexity, where we both know a more secretive variety of the elegance of nature exists.

"Where were we?" Alba is the first to emerge from our trance.

I just look at her.

"I think it's time to join Rob and start talking about the project." She collects her stuff quickly and gets up, leaving me to rush and put away the slides in my container. Mixed up, for sure.

The Scientist

*

When we join Rob, he is already sitting at the round table in his office with an empty cup next to him. Denyse serves some more coffee for the three of us as Alba and I sit down.

Rob speaks quickly, with a slight tone of anxiety: 'Well, what do you think, Alba?"

"You can relax, Rob. No need to convince me. In general, I'm quite excited at the potential of this project. Naturally I have some specific questions." Her tone is firm, rather categorical.

"Go on, let's hear them." Rob looks alert and ready.

"First, I need to know why do you need that expensive piece of equipment, the confocal microscope. I saw slides that had very many images of neurons. Can't you do with the current microscopes?"

Rob looks at me for an explanation, even if he knows the answer for sure.

"The images you have seen, Dr Gruber—" "Call me Alba. It's quicker."

"Right, Alba, the images you saw were from an ordinary fluorescent microscope, the pictures taken from different focal points each time. So you focus on a certain depth of the sample and take a picture. Then you focus more deeply and take another, and so on, many times."

"But why do you need to see the sample at different depths?" Alba looks at me first, then at Rob.

So he replies: "There are different structures at different depths. Some change quite subtly with maturation and disease."

"Yes," I add, "our diagnostic capacity would be greatly increased. We could discriminate much better if we had the whole picture in 3D."

"But why does this type of microscope cost so much?" Alba finally reveals her concern.

"Because we take many different photos with one focus distant from the next by only 0.2 microns, then we need to reconstitute the whole picture, and that in turn can only be done by computer power. A large box of electronics plus a laser and an SGI computer are part and parcel of this equipment."

I take out a brochure from my folder and give it to her: "Have a look at it in your own time."

"Rob, would there be any objection in listing this equipment, if we buy it, as an asset of my company?"

I see that the question has taken Rob by surprise, so I ask: "And what is your company's name, Alba?"

"If all goes well, it will be called CoDis Limited, short for CoDiscovery, which is what I'm hoping the four of you will be able to do."

"Who are the other three?"

"I've selected a group in the John Curtin School of Medical Research at the ANU, and another in the Division of Entomology at CSIRO, but am still looking for the fourth one. Do you have any suggestions to make?"

Rob, in the meantime, has found an answer for her:

"You know, Alba, I think it's quite legitimate to list that piece of equipment in your company's asset book. Then you can lease it to us for the duration of the project."

"Right. But that actually increases the cost of your project. I'll have to ask our accountant as to the best way to structure this research agreement."

A strange new dynamic is setting among us. Alba appears to be playing a straight you-need-me card with Rob, whilst more of a we-need-each-other game with me. He seems unruffled by this and by the way our relative position has been levelling since Alba's project entered the scene. Still I am uneasy. I have the impression of being led, not exactly in a direction I don't want to go, but certainly at a pace I'm not used to. Alba looks like she is the bearer of an irrepressible agenda, proceeding undeterred regardless of what everyone else thinks. A strong woman, for sure. I've met very few others like her in the past and my mind goes to Carol.

"I do have a candidate for the fourth slot!" I am quite excited by the idea:

"Her name is Professor Carol Latimar, a very competent scientist. We worked together while I did my post-doc and we remained in touch."

"What's her area?"

"Inflammation of the mucosae leading to cancer."

"Right, yes, cancer would complement nicely our portfolio. We have neurodegenerative disease here, juvenile diabetes from the John Curtin and new antibiotics from Entomology. A good fit, I'd say, if she has a good project. Thank you, James. Could you ring the details to my secretary, Debbie?"

"Sure, and do you want me to test the water with Carol?"

"I can do that," Rob interjects "I see Carol regularly at the University Senate meetings and one is scheduled for the day after tomorrow."

"Perfect. Now, let's see: I have your project proposal. I've shown it to my Chairman and he's happy with it. I'll give the figures to my accountant. I've lined up the lawyers for drafting the Memorandum of Understanding. So we are quite well placed. Your project is the most advanced for the purpose of drafting. Any questions?"

"Alba, you said to me that your company would be floated in a backdoor listing. What's that?" Rob shows some concern.

"It's a quicker way to list our company on the Stock Exchange. We take over another company that is already listed there, one that has sold its operations and is only a cash box."

"Who is in charge of this company now?" Rob asks.

"Two directors: one is a lawyer, the other was a mining executive."

"Would you retain them on your Board?" Rob pursues.

"Yes, they would be on our Board, since they would end up with fifteen per cent of the joint company. Don't worry, Rob; it's all been under Paul's scrutiny for months now. Surely you know Paul Creagan? He is going to be the Chairman, and wouldn't be in it to be drawn into some unsavoury deal."

"So you'd be the CEO, he the Chairman, both of you on the Board of Directors with those two other characters. Who else?" Rob keeps on.

"A bank executive, a woman with a Ph.D. in physics who's very interested in scientific developments, and another doctor who just retired from a major computer group with a bundle."

Rob drops his stare and looks at his blank note pad.

So I ask: "Alba, you have given us three years. Do you think that's enough?"

"We'd encourage you to do it in that time frame, so there would be a premium for early events. But of course we are realistic and have planned to raise from the share issue enough money for longer."

Rob has managed to write some notes and emerges from his pad: "Ok, what do you need from us next, Alba?"

"I'd like you to start instructing your lawyers to work with ours and agree on the Research Agreements. The four separate agreements will represent the exclusive assets of the Company, on the basis of which we'll raise the funds."

"How much?"

"Between twelve and fourteen million dollars."

*

Money, that money; the single currency may have carried a different value for each of us at the time. In hindsight, I flash up this thought of mine under an artistic, artificial light. I imagine Rob feeling the freer flow of money, the kind he used to touch once upon a time in America; Lucky Jim tingled by a sense of transgression for how keen he was on the money and on the woman behind it. Then I see Alba boarding her new vessel which would ferry science across to the wider world again, and not for the last time.

The artifice fades quickly away from my mind, though. Now the differential among us disappears and I see our trio marching ahead together with a joint purpose.

***

Four

3 May 1996. Not that I needed an official excuse to have the Latimars here for lunch, but I mentioned the renovations, completed at last: did they want to see the final result? Of course, yes.

So I've shopped, cooked, and thought a lot: what can I say to Carol to convince her to accept Alba's offer? Martina is in Melbourne, but Joan and Max are here and welcome the idea of Eve coming too. They are good friends.

Ok, let's concentrate on the mixed roast. According to mother, it's better to carve it early and put the slices back on the tray and in the warm oven again. Done. The vegetables are already laid down and roasted; the oven has all the trays full. Let's close it now.

Carol said she'd bring a mixed salad; Martina made her special *cenci* before she left, so everything is under control. I drop on the couch in the living room and look outside. Joan and Max went out for a walk with Matilda, our three-year-old sheepdog, and left the front door open. We do it regularly when we are home: that way, our terrace house at the end of The Esplanade seems to continue on to the park and the beach beyond.

We built the table next to the bay window for the view, just one column/leg, with the other head side attached to the wall. It's one of the new features and really my own idea. Martina thought it looked like some table on a boat and that's exactly why I wanted it this way.

"Hi, Jim." Carol is the first to enter with her bowl.

"Oh, you're here. Didn't see you coming in."

"Yeh. Mark is trying to find a parking spot and Eve is playing with Max and Matilda, and Joan, of course."

"Let's put your salad in the kitchen. Are you well?"

"Yeh, yeh; tired, of course. I spent hours last night finishing off some papers due on Monday. Still have experiments to write up; my students seem to drop down one notch every year . . . ."

"Are you sure you're not becoming more and more demanding?"

"Could be." She looks pensive and worried.

"Hi, Mark, did you find a park?" I'm relieved he's here.

"Lucky, really, that someone decided to leave me his car spot. How are things? It looks great here! I like the new floor."

"Tasmanian oak." I remember how difficult it was to find a large number of boards all the same colour and length.

"And the table—fantastic!"

"I'm glad you like it. I had to fight quite hard for it."

The kids arrive.

"Hi, Eve. You're well? You seem breathless."

"They ran, Dad." Joan, at fifteen, is the oldest and treats Eve, thirteen, and Max, at twelve, as children.

"Carol, would you like to see the extensions upstairs?"

"I would too," says Mark, who pushes Max in front of him. Joan takes Carol upstairs and lets her go first.

"You are not going, Eve?" Obviously not, she is sitting down.

"I've seen it already; Max's shown it to me the other day when I came with some friends to the beach."

"Do you like what we've done?" I ask.

"Yeah, there is much more room now for Max, and you, of course."

"Yes, Martina and I have the top floor for ourselves and Max has his own room at last. He must be really pleased."

"And I quite like your new balcony. Great view!"

"Actually, the view there is filtered through the top of the trees; so there is less water view from upstairs than down here. Down here there are only the tree trunks between our view and the sea. But on the balcony, if you sit there at dawn and the sky starts colouring, you feel like you're surrounded by a powerful cosmic change."

"I've never heard you talking of cosmic changes! It sounds poetical." She looks at me.

"What do I normally talk about? With you, I mean."

"You never talk to me. Like all adults, you just ask questions."

"Would you like me to?"

"Yes, when you talk with my parents you say things that I like. But you never talk with me. I'm too young, of course."

"Ok, I'll take that on board." I see the others coming downstairs and get up.

"What do you think?" I ask Mark.

"Well, I'll leave the aesthetic comments to Carol, but on the technical side I'm impressed. Going up one floor and finding support from the sloping ground, the metal bridge over the rocks, I find that really ingenious."

"You'll be amused," Carol steps in, "but you know the particular item I like? The yellow rubber floor in your bathroom with the beautiful pattern raised to avoid slipping."

"Martina's idea, of course." I say, a little disappointed.

"And in your new bedroom one feels like in a mountain retreat, comfortable and away from everything else."

"That was the idea," I say. "Ready for a drink?"

*

The lunch has gone very smoothly. When the woman of the house is not there, everyone helps and the joint effort seems immune to criticism. At the moment, Joan and Max are in the kitchen putting together their surprise dessert. I thought we'd just have Martina's *cenci*.

"Here it is!" Joan walks towards the table carrying a strange construct on a plate and Max follows with a bowl of mixed berries.

"What is it?" asks Carol. "I've never seen it before!"

"It's *cartellati*, a sweet that a friend's grandmother makes. We used Mum's *cenci* and fried them in honey with a little cinnamon this morning. When they cool down, the *cenci* glue together in the shape you've chosen. Ours is like the coil of a shell." Joan and Max seem very satisfied with the result.

"I want to meet this grandmother," says Mark. "It's a great new taste, soft and crunchy at the same time. Quite different."

Carol has been quiet throughout the lunch, not her usual self. Now the *cartellati* seem to have moved her.

"Yes, I think we need more sweetness in our lives," she says.

I look at her, uncertain. We've been friends for almost fifteen years but she still surprises me at times.

"Carol, why don't you accept Dr Gruber's offer?"

"Simple, no more work. I'm exhausted."

"But the additional staff would help, surely," I insist.

"It's not the bench work, of course. It's the supervising, the writing up, the responsibility . . . Only I can do that." She looks dispirited.

"Carol is one of those women," Mark intervenes, "and apparently there are many, who can't prioritize her work. Everything is equally important. And she takes on some duties that are really of dubious benefit."

"Such as?" Carol's tone is sepulchral.

"Such as your honorary positions: Chair of committees after committees. What's the good of that?" Mark seems to settle a long-delayed question.

"Why do you both see this project as so good for me?" She is directing her point to Mark and me, but I'm happy to let Mark answer:

"Because the upside is clear—two million dollars in three years—while there is no downside whatsoever."

"Mark is right, Carol," I add. "If one of your research project, funded by the NH&MRC, doesn't work, you have no papers published and your reputation is tarnished. But with this, if it doesn't work, nothing happens. Everyone knows that R&D projects are risky and speculative; the analysts give it a chance of success of one in ten."

"And what happens if it does succeed?" Eve enters the conversation.

"If it goes well, there may be a new way of preventing cancer in the bowel, for instance. Not a bad result, eh?" I reply.

"Mum, that's important: more than any of your committees. Why are you so stubborn?" Eve must have heard this phrase often.

"What's more, Carol, I need you there," I say.

"Why?" Carol is angry, a good sign that she is at least reacting to what we are saying.

"Because the whole program will be managed by us, the four project leaders. You and I can support each other if we need to."

"Have you already signed the agreement?" Carol asks me.

"No, there won't be an agreement unless all four are on board. And your refusal would raise suspicion in the other two. You are well known for your integrity. They might think there is something fishy about the Company if you refuse."

"Well, I'll think about it while Mark may analyze my committee duties and prioritize them as only a male brain can do?" Carol seems more relaxed now.

"Why wouldn't a female brain prioritize, Dad?" Eve seems keen.

"I didn't say that, but women have communication structures in their brain that allow them to do more than one thing at the same time. If they did prioritize effectively, they wouldn't be able to do this so easily. Isn't it so, Jim?"

"More or less. Women's brains have evolved somewhat differently from men's, of course, and in most cases it is an advantage. But not if someone can't say no to more and more duties."

"How can one learn to prioritize, from the point of view of neurology?" Eve seems to be really interested, as she has remained at the table while Joan and Max have gone out.

"I don't think you can change the architecture of your brain to that extent, but there are practical tricks one can use." I'm glad we are moving to a more general topic.

"Such as?" Eve presses on.

"Well, for example, you can draw up a table with various tasks that you are normally involved in. To each task you assign a weight: high if that duty is important to you, lower for those that have lesser meaning. Each week you sum up your activities; a successful week is one where you reach your goal, say three hundred, with a small number of tasks. That means you've been focusing on important tasks only; you have prioritized successfully."

"That sounds easy." Eve gets up and joins Max in the park.

***

Five

2 October 2015. On this day in 1996, Alba's company came into existence. It was listed on the Stock Exchange as CoDis Limited, having raised twelve and a half million dollars from institutional and private investors. The share issue was considered successful—although at the lower end of expectations—and with the other money from the original cash box, the Company now had a reserve of over fifteen million dollars, a substantial sum for R&D at the time.

At home preparing material for my book, I look at the papers I have scattered on the carpet of a spare room that is used as an archive: the Prospectus, the articles in various newspapers, the photos and, in a separate envelope, Alba's speech.

I remember she organized a function that day at her new office in our Institute building. She had rented several rooms on the tenth floor, a largely empty space at the time. The logo of her company was imprinted on the glass entrance door, an elegant logo designed by graphic house Billy Blue. It was a sort of get-together of all the people involved, from the Board of Directors to the financial institution that had underwritten the issue, the research groups that were now part of the joint venture and the new staff of the Company.

I got there early with Rob and started meeting people. The Chairman, Paul Creagan was easily the tallest one in the room. A puffy face under white hair, he was an affable guy who grabbed my hand and promised me it would be a great adventure. The other woman on the Board, the physicist/banker, who was wearing an extraordinarily tight suit, looked at me through blue eyes that seemed unusually distanced and declared herself honoured to be associated again with the bright minds of academia.

The director with a computer background, and the bundle of money he made with that, was a very thin man with a pointed nose and cobalt-blue eyes who told me that his role was to watch us and prevent derailments.

Then I met the two directors who came from the previous, listed company. I try to recall my first impression but the only thing I remember was my strong dislike of them both straight away. Roth Cooper was the lawyer, a sort of dandy with oily brown hair, pointed shoes and a very narrow tie. He told me that he was very disappointed: after the first hour of trading the share price, issued at $1.00, had peaked at $1.28 and had then fallen rapidly. He believed it could go below par by the end of the day's session. His mate, Joel Patricks, was the former mining executive and former miner, with a reddish round face in which the eyes played little part and a mouth with barely drawn lips. He declared that he understood very little of what we were doing but surely hoped we would make his money multiply.

Then I met the director of research, Lyanne Davies. A small, thin woman with very short black hair, she seemed to me all nerve and energy as she told me how much she was looking forward to working with me. With a stretchy smile, she described the computer program she had devised to keep track of milestones in our projects: a plan that I took as a threat.

I didn't speak with Alba, nor with the financial people she was entertaining, but chatted with Carol and the other two project leaders. Carol knew Leon Kelly, the senior researcher of the John Curtin School, a large man with a very good disposition and obvious Irish drinking habits. A generous, vivid intelligence, he seemed to be the easiest going of the three: someone who wouldn't create problems.

The fourth scientist, the entomologist from the CSIRO, was a nervous, short and round guy who struck me immediately as painfully ambitious. John Harvey, an Englishman who had spent only the previous five years in Australia in the cocoon shelter of Canberra, had a number of facial tics, but all very mild. So you had to pay a lot of attention if you wanted to define them. He said to me, without much grace, that the only thing he was concerned about was the pace of our "medical projects". His would surely be delivering quickly, having to do only with "bugs and chemistry".

At this point the Chairman asked for our attention and said that Alba would start her address. We all gathered in the entrance hall in a semicircle around where she stood, with the letters **CoDis Ltd** glued on to the back wall.

Should I put here the whole or part of Alba's speech? I've given a lot of thought to this question. A summary perhaps? That would betray her intention to show how inclusive she had become, how she had mastered the jargons and penetrated the mindsets of a disparate assembly. There were financiers and accountants, shareholders and scientists. All had to be convinced that she understood each of them with their quirks and objectives.

As Alba addressed us, it seemed that she had thought of everything: of the security of mind that a pot of cash can buy; of the confidence that check-points at every corner can give; of the probability of success with a fine portfolio of projects; of the reliability that credible scientists offer; of the fine positioning of our projects in the Research and Development chain. Only the long speech can convey how much she invested in this venture, with reason and passion.

Thank you Paul. The idea of this venture came to us as we talked about the difficulties encountered by the Biotechnology Industry in Australia. "As a pioneer of this industry," Paul said to me, "you should have a good idea of what works and what doesn't."

We soon came to the conclusion that one of the main problems was management. How do you manage R&D in a way that it is of the highest scientific quality, cognizant of the variability in life sciences, sympathetic to the character of researchers who are, almost inevitably, thinkers with the highest sense of individualism and independence? How do you do all this in a restricted time frame?

"You have an MBA," Paul told me "I'm only an accountant, who's become a professional chairman, and can steer finance, but not management. Think about it."

I did. "First," I said, "prepare to raise double the money you think we need." In this industry, there is nothing worse than being taken by the fear of running out of money before the project is finished. And the project always lasts longer than you thought. But if you are lucky and your budget was indeed realistic, there are so many unfinished projects out there that with your spare funds you can always acquire some and double overnight your business base. That's the money side. As for the business model, ours is original but only in that it mixes and crosses two separate models that, in different fields, have been very successful. One is peer review in the research field. Before publication, research articles are vetted by peers who can judge if they are worth publishing not only on the basis of rules that have to be followed, but also on the basis of what each of the peers considers to be original, yet congruent with existing science.

Crossed with the peer review model, I inserted best practice in management, a set of planning and reporting rules that are well known to deliver results and accountability. To put the two models together, there will be management meetings where all four research leaders will judge the quarterly results of only one of them each time and make constructive criticism to develop it further. Our Director of Research will follow all the projects on a continuous basis and I will participate in each management meeting. But enough on method.

In my spare room now, I look at the length of the business part of her speech and find that's much shorter than the second, the one where she talks about research. This reveals quite clearly her preference, but it is odd, because at the time she seemed to us to be engaged mostly in the business side of things. Perhaps she wanted to give us the impression of a hard chief executive who wouldn't be swayed by her passion for science.

Perhaps business was not a natural medium for her, and whilst she had mastered its language, her heart was not in it. I had noticed her stilted monologues when she was explaining those matters to us sometimes, as if the effort put hurdles on the natural flow of her words.

Strangely, I feel more affection for that business persona—hard working against her grain and fighting external counter-currents—who, now I know, was fragile and in danger. From this distant time, I also know that her natural passion for science would survive anything and that she would go on, thanks to that drive, ever stronger, without my help. But let's go back to her speech:

Let's talk about the more exciting stuff, the research. You've read in the Prospectus the basic story of our four projects. Of course we've been very neutral in their description there, for obvious reasons. Here, let me be speculative, let me be optimistic, let me dream.

They are four gems of ideas that have already come some way. From concept to project, with all the practical qualities of aims and milestones. Projects that have people behind them, who think and work at the bench, people who criticise them and people who construct. People who want to participate in research adventures. This is what the four projects have in common. Now let's see them one at the time.

The Entomology project is, of course, about insects, but no ordinary insects. Our group will venture to the tropical north of Australia and collect rare specimens. Insects are peculiar, anyway, for their immunity to various pathogens they carry. Think of the organism that causes malaria, the parasite that a particular mosquito carries in her belly without affecting her viability, except for making her more thirsty and dangerous to humans. Think of the other mosquito that carries, without consequences for herself, the virus of encephalitis. These insects must have mechanisms in their bodies to protect them. By looking for insects where no one else had done systematic studies, our people at Entomology can collect them and analyze their biochemistry.

John Harvey will be searching for special chemicals, potions that have been secretly doing their protective jobs for millions of years, and discover perhaps new kinds of antibiotics. As you'd know, there are few antibiotics around and attempts to find novel ones are rare nowadays.

From insects to juvenile diabetes. I don't need to describe the disease that attacks young lives in their daily reality, but want to throw a magic wand at it. Our well-known immunologist from the John Curtin School at the ANU had this idea: since the disease is due to an autoimmune dysfunction—our own immune cells destroying our pancreas—why not try to trick the immune system back to normal?

For example, try to distract it with the immune work it must carry on when injected with the potent vaccine for Q Fever? If we can interrupt in time the destruction of the pancreatic cells that produce insulin, perhaps the diabetes will never set itself in. That's what Leon Kelly wants to try, with mice first, and then hopefully with young people. The vaccine is safe and in use already. If only can it do a little more than protect against Q Fever, and stop the immune cells from finishing to destroy their pancreas!

Another of our projects is on the preventative side of cancer. Carol Latimar has been looking at the various changes in the mucosae lining the lung and the gut of individuals <u>before</u> they develop cancer. There in the deep entrails of our organism, immune cells, again, start inflaming the mucosae for one or other reason. In the long term, the inflammation and the repair mechanisms that it ensues may fail, turning to malignant growth. If we are able to assess early on this state of chronic inflammation, we would give a warning that it is better to act, treat it and stop the process in time.

The fourth, but clearly not the least of our projects, is in the area of neuroscience and right here at the Boyle Institute. James Corsini will be the proud recipient of important equipment that will allow him to study, at different depths, neuronal growth in various patients by using simple nasal biopsies.

In people who show early symptoms of neurological disorders, these biopsies might reveal in 3D, under the famous microscope, patterns of growth that would identify very early on the type of disease that is developing. It is the diagnostic potential that is so very promising in this project, an exciting project for us. In summary, we could achieve a step forward for the:

Discovery of new antibiotics from insects.
Immunisation against juvenile diabetes.
Prevention of solid cancers in the mucosae.
Diagnostics for neurological diseases.

I said a step forward because our role, still ambitious, is only to move the projects from the safe haven of the laboratory to the initial stage of clinical trials. If we are successful, we are going to add value to our projects and will be ready to hand them over to the specialists of the next stage.

If successful, we will have operated the transition, or if you like, the translation from science to medicine, from laboratory animals to humans. And that will have happened thanks to our competence, but also to your trust and support. Now let's hope we'll be lucky too.

Many people stayed after her speech, seemingly creating a moment of entente, all elements of the enterprise reunited: the fuel, the talent and the perseverance, all in the same room for the first time. I saw two financiers talking with Leon, who seemed excited by their questions; Harvey chatting laboriously with an accountant who listened without a word; Lyanne Davies with a chastised look in front of Carol's authority; Alba, pale now and clearly exhausted. I approached her as soon as I could:

"That was a success already, to have tied us all together. Are you ready to relax and be complimented?"

"Thank you. Yes, I should relax and enjoy the roll-out. I wish I could."

Unsettled a moment ago, her eyes paused on me, tentatively at first, then trusting, as if wanting to rest in my care.

***

Six

18 January 1997. It's the day before the end of our summer holidays.

I have decided to go to the lab for a few hours to organize our work; the first day is usually quite slack and I want to make up for that. The last two months of last year were rather confusing as we tried to accommodate the new project into our main program. Rob was quite concerned that we couldn't fill the expectations of CoDis, so he intervened personally to choose the new personnel and insisted on remaining our *trait-d'union* with Alba, thus complicating my plans.

Now all that is out of our way and things should settle. Today I want to make sure that they do and plan to check on our plan for the next few months, up to the management meeting on the 7th of April, when our project will be discussed.

While at my desk, the phone rings; it's Paul Creagan, CoDis' Chairman.

"Happy new year, Jim. Already at work?"

"Thank you, same to you. Yes, I like to prepare work for my staff the day before they come back from their holidays."

"Jim, the reason I'm calling is to ask you if we can get together today. I know it's far too short notice, but I had to come to town to get the mail and Alba will join us before going to work herself. Would that be possible?"

"No problem. I can come back here later."

"Would 11.30 suit you? I'm in my office in Martin Place."

"Fine. See you there."

I've had few dealings with Paul so I can't imagine what he wants. I should have asked. My impression of him is that of a mild man, too experienced to be aggressive but also one who's been fortunate enough in his business to have escaped cynicism. In fact I'm glad he called me; I'd like to know him better. I read in the CoDis Prospectus of his background in accounting and his fostering of many small companies.

I take the train to Martin Place and find his building easily. It's one of the oldest, there for at least two generations. The lift squeaks as it takes me to the 10th floor and opens to a small hall with narrow corridors left and right. Paul's office is on the left a short distance away. I see, through glass walls, a largish room packed with filing cabinets and desks, machines of all sorts, and one old computer, all lit by neon lights that seem to cover the whole ceiling and brighten also the space outside the room. A grey-haired woman in a brown-patterned dress comes to the door to greet me.

"Paul is on the phone. Do come in. How are you, Dr Corsini? I'm Patricia, Paul's PA."

She lets me sit on a visitor chair facing an empty desk and offers coffee or tea.

"Or perhaps a glass of cold water, with a day like this when we should all be in our swimming costumes?"

"Good idea, Patricia. Thank you. I was at work anyway."

She manoeuvres around a photocopier and I see the door of a small fridge sticking out when she opens it and disappearing again soon after.

"Here it is." She pours water from a small bottle, some for me and some for herself, with a familiarity that reveals long service in that office.

"Paul has spoken about you in terms that are quite complimentary, if I may say so, Dr Corsini. He thinks you are the most reasonable of the four scientists and one with whom he feels comfortable to talk."

"Oh, thanks. That's mutual."

"I'm glad to hear that, Jim." Paul has opened the door and invites me into his office, a room of reasonable size with black leather armchairs

54

and couch, a desk and a circular table all packed in with a sense of functional discipline.

"You can see that there is nothing superfluous here; this is a working place where few people come. Most of the time I go and visit associates in their own premises." He speaks with a benevolent tone and a baritone voice which has occasional changes of pitch and a rhythm that reminds me of Irish dancing.

"Alba is going to join us soon, Jim. In the meantime, let me explain why I've called you. I'd like you to understand this business of ours a bit more: perhaps you have questions, perhaps you haven't heard enough. To be frank, I see you as a second intermediary, in addition to Alba, between the business and the scientists.

"There may be occasions when the other team leaders will have doubts or reservations that they won't express to Alba. Then it could be up to you to explain and resolve the hitch. Is this something you can and would want to do?"

"I don't have any problem with that, if it's all above board."

"Of course, and Alba concurs. You see, she'll be very busy this year; she has to respond routinely to shareholders' queries, to the Stock Exchange, to institutional investors. I can do only so much and then the scientific context stops me."

"Why did you get involved in a project that is so far away from your practice?"

"My practice, as you call it, is simply mechanics; it's accounting that applies to a whole lot of areas, each of them quite remote from my own. I've specialized in what you may call a common denominator. All areas of business have to obey to certain rules: planning budgets, deploying funds and reporting. No one escapes, scientists included."

"But I believe you were involved also in fund-raising."

"Exactly. And in that sense you are right. I became a bit of an entrepreneur myself, but that was because I wanted to help Alba in her quest."

"Why?"

"I had invested my own funds in her previous ventures and grew to respect her commitment and integrity. Of course I also made a profit out of them."

"But in this you became the major proponent of CoDis' business."

"That's right. You can imagine my network of contacts, my personal friendships, my being known by institutional investors and so on. I've put all this at CoDis' disposal."

"So who owns the Company now?"

"There are about five hundred shareholders. The major ones are the previous directors, institutional investors, and then many wealthy individuals. This is a speculative stock, so it wasn't suitable for mums and dads. I've invested my own funds in it."

"And do you think Dr Gruber is good at shareholders' relations?"

"Together with me, yes. But what investors want to know is how competent she is, how committed and honest she continues to be in the long run. And on that score I have absolute confidence. In my long career as Chairman of the Board, I've never met anyone so diligent, so scrupulous and attentive to the business. The only problem, perhaps, is that she does it as if her life depended on it."

"Why is that a problem?"

"Because she may become emotional about it and lose her cool. I need to prevent that at all costs. And here I think you can help."

"I don't understand how I could do that."

"Say, if you get close and more intimate with CoDis' business, you may be able to shield her from at least the scientific problems that may arise. What I'd like to achieve is you becoming a buffer for her from your own groups as I do the same from the business side of things. The pressure within, of running a company, is enough. Alba doesn't need to be open to attacks from without."

"Ah, you'll have the bigger job there. I don't think there will be much of a scientist attack."

"No, of course science has different qualities from business. But I'm referring more to what scientists may <u>not</u> do, than what they might do.

In other words, the pressure will come from not delivering. I need you to help there."

"We were given at least three years."

"Yes, sure. But even the perception of slow delivery may be enough for certain operators to play with the share price and manipulate the market. Small companies with a pot of cash are very vulnerable in that sense."

"Vulnerable? Are we vulnerable?" Alba has arrived and enters the room directly. She is wearing a white linen suit that flatters her light summer tan, which bears a dark rose tint reminiscent of an American Indian.

"You know market manipulators, don't you?" Paul doesn't seem to feel the impact of her presence, but I have to have a gulp of water to recompose.

"So have you two explained everything?" Her voice has a joking, relaxed tone.

"I don't know if Jim has it all clear." Paul seems less anxious than before and his question has the sense of a rhetorical statement.

"Sort of, but perhaps I should ask Alba some clarification."

"Go ahead." She looks amused.

"What do you think I should do to encourage the other team leaders to make superior efforts to deliver early?" My intention is irony but she doesn't get it.

"Ideally, the four of you should have a private meeting before our management meetings so that you can prime them. I mean, knowing better than them the Company's objectives, you would be able to explain difficult things to them so that they would be more easygoing and less confrontational with me. I know that if we work together—that is always in the same direction—without undue resistance, delivery will be easier."

"OK, I can try, but I'm not sure it will work."

"Shall we continue this conversation over lunch? Sorry, Jim, I didn't mention that I invited Alba here for lunch. You'd be most welcome if you could join us." Paul gets up, assuming I'll accept, which I do.

We walk up to and then along Macquarie Street to reach Paul's club, The Australian. While Paul signs the register, Alba takes me aside in the dark hall.

"I'm afraid you will be taken only to the mixed dining room where women are admitted. The other one is more exclusive."

That doesn't worry me. I'm more interested in the art works that are hung along the corridors. Quite remarkable stuff. Wood panels cover most walls and create a hushed atmosphere, dark and traditional, where the brightness of Alba's figure stands out like a white orchid.

She has an ironic look on her face as the waiter leads us to our table and asks Paul if he'll have his usual red. But Alba begs to differ and I follow her on Pinot Gris.

"Are you two ganging up on me?" Paul seems very relaxed, but it's a false impression.

With mild manners he traps Alba into a relentless conversation about reports and disclosures, trips to Melbourne, presentations to major investors, main targets and subtle ways to publicize effectively the Company. I understand only half of it and concentrate on their body language. Paul's is very attentive, with his blue eyes fixed on Alba one moment, then moving them to a notepad where he writes with amazing speed. There is a sense of asynchrony between the talking and the writing, as if Paul wrote down something else from what they are saying. Perhaps reminders of something more for later.

"Remember, Alba, that at the presentation in Melbourne you'll have to be inspiring. We—bean counters, you'd say—as investors in CoDis, want to hear of an uplifting future, one where the profit is obviously there (it would be mayhem if it wasn't) but where we can contribute to some worthwhile cause. You need to project the applications of our research in a way that elevates the game to a realistic, yet lofty horizon."

"Sure, Paul, I know. Our research program is very realistic. As for a higher purpose, there is nothing I like better than to talk about magic discoveries, new remedies, deeper understanding of nature's laws, opening frontiers, a changing paradigm for linking science to business . . ."

"OK, let me see what you have in mind. Write a few pages so that I can check and correct if necessary; you know how sensitive and tricky it is. We wouldn't want to mislead our audience."

Our lunch doesn't last long, served as it is just a few minutes after our ordering, over one glass of wine and obvious signs of affection between Alba and Paul.

"You two seem to be working well together," I say at the end of the meal.

"It's the affinity that comes to veterans of the stock market," says Paul. "It's the camaraderie that is built while going to war for the same flag: entrepreneurship."

Once downstairs and outside, we say goodbye to Paul. Alba is going to drive me to the lab and I farewell him with a new sense of esteem for a good man who considers many facets of the game and respects the different players with equanimity. A man without pretensions but with a clear idea of what his role as chairman means: ultimate responsibility for what happens to the Company and its shareholders' investment in it.

Alba emerges from the parking station in a manual Lancia Delta, which approaches me all revved up.

"Don't they make them automatic?" I ask while getting in.

"They do, but not for me. I like to feel the needs of the car, change gears myself when I hear it revving high; I like to be in touch with its rhythm rather than being driven without knowing."

"Do you feel this way for other things? Or for human machines?"

"Yes, starting from myself. To know is a passion; really it gives me great pleasure. Other people are moved by mystery. I'm moved only because that pushes me to want to know."

"Does that apply to others? I mean their wish to know. I know so little about you."

"Well, you need to make an effort for that. I wouldn't want to preempt your curiosity. What would you like to know?"

"Everything. But let's start with your family, if I may: your current one."

"A bit blunt, don't you think? Can you rephrase it to encourage me to answer?"

"OK. You seem to me to be very free with your time, as if nothing existed outside your work."

"That's better. Yes, I have a lot of free time and that's because my husband is often away and our son, who is eighteen, is quite independent and very happy to do his own things."

"So do you work hard to fill up time?"

"Not at all. Work is for me a passion and a pleasure. The kind of work I do, of course. And I've planned this particular venture for over a year with Paul."

"Why? What's the attraction?"

"I've always been attracted by the sophisticated design of nature in biology: billions of years of evolution to rest on designs that are efficient and economical. You know, I remember being struck by a recent report of the structure of a particular sponge, the deep-sea sponge. It lives on the dark ocean floor and yet it builds by itself from the sand a skeleton made of tiny glass structures. And all that at cold temperatures, not with the fire that glass makers use in their workshops."

"And what do sponges do with their glass things?"

"Optical fibers. They've been making them for sixty million years."

"But what do they do with optical fibers when they live in darkness at the bottom of the ocean?"

"That's their currency. They produce optical fibers to exchange them in a symbiotic way with bioluminescent bacteria, which need the fibers to shine their light through."

"And what do the sponges get in return?"

"Well, there is a third partner, a shrimp. What happens is that the bacteria form a crown on top of the sponge and their illuminated fibers attract other marine life to the darkness. Then the shrimps feed on that life and their waste feeds the sponge, and the bacteria, of course."

"Nice arrangement. But what you are talking about is nature and science. I can't see the nexus with your job."

"I see nature as a hidden jewel and scientists as explorers and discoverers who bring the jewel out in its splendor. But I see the job unfinished. What is the worth of the gem? I like to think that it depends on us, on what we do with it. Should we just look at it and be amazed? Or is it an example we can copy or mimic, using its sophisticated design as a pattern we can reproduce?"

"So, in your mind I am an explorer and a discoverer. And what are you?"

"I am the one who allows you to do all that, then I can take the gem and the strategy behind it to the point where it becomes beneficial. You see, I am not content with knowing how things are, how complex and sophisticated nature has been able to refine them. I want to transport them to the right place, the place of need. The place where they can be of benefit, not just being."

"That's seeing nature as a pattern, as an example of what can be done, of what it has done for a long time. You want to know, through us scientists, how it can be reproduced without destroying it, isn't that it?"

"Exactly, and I'm on a mission for this."

"Is it why you went into a trance when I showed you that slide of neurons and fibers?"

"Yes, but there was something else then, something more personal."

"May I ask what?"

"When you showed me that slide, the memory of my studies lit up. I went back to my neurology courses and strangely, because a long time had passed, I dived straight back into my memory of neurons and how they fired. I went down from level to level, from the microscopic to the atomic, and marveled at my capacity to dive and remember.

Then I noticed that you were there, diving with me. It was as if you were already inside my memory, meeting me down there. It was really weird."

Alba stops the car and turns silent, putting her hand on the gear stick once more. I touch her hand lightly, to confirm that meeting, to assure her that I was really there then and am with her now.

Walking together from the car park to our building, Alba remains silent, perhaps sorry to have said too much or still dealing with her own revelation. I won't say a word either, taking in the events of a day that was quite remarkable.

***

Seven

3-5 February 1997. "Hi, Jim, it's Alba." The phone selects a higher pitch and her voice sounds girlish. "Just wanted to let you know that I haven't forgotten your memo."

"Oh, it was just to try to understand how you got interested in the insect project." Mine was a short memo, or rather, an excuse.

"Yes, that's it. I have an article here that I cut out years ago. It will show you where I come from in this particular interest."

"Can I come up to get it?"

"No, no. I'm rushing to catch a plane. I'll give it to Debbie and she'll take it downstairs later. Ok, see you."

I find the idea of her leaving a bit depressing, but fortunately one of my Ph.D. students walks in and takes me into a complex technical discussion. An hour or so later, Debbie knocks at the door.

"Good morning, Jim." She brings the article Alba mentioned. "It's the original, so she'd like to have it back." Debbie's tone is kind, and compared to Denyse, she seems more helpful.

"Will she be back for the management meeting?" I ask.

"Oh yes, she wouldn't miss that. She's only going to be away in Canberra for one of her advisory roles." Debbie seems happy to talk about her boss.

"Does she go there often?"

"Yes, every fortnight. She has three advisory positions in different government departments at the moment."

"Can she afford to do that, now that she heads a public company?"

"Of course. It's very useful: more networking, you know. From the other members of the boards or councils, Alba gets to hear more news than by reading all the press in the morning."

"Have you worked with her long?"

"On and off for ten years."

"What is she like? As a boss, I mean."

"She's the most interesting boss I've had. Always on something new, always different and unexpected. And I love working here. All these young, unconventional people!"

"And Alba? How does she feel about it? She doesn't seem exactly in her natural environment."

"I don't thing a natural environment exists for her."

"So where does she fit?"

"Nowhere: not at home, not in the office, not in departmental meetings. She said to me she feels at ease only while travelling from one place to the other. Only in between places. She calls herself the woman of the interface."

*

A couple of days later I find the time to read the article, an hour or so before the meeting scheduled for that afternoon. It will be our first management meeting and we'll gather to discuss the entomology project. The article that prompted Alba's interest in the field was written in early 1990 by a certain Sandy Rumi.

Insects: Reversing a Negative impression

Insects? Buzzing, biting, stinging, crawling come to mind.
Any pleasant thoughts? A colourful butterfly.
Up to a million species and few positive things to say about insects.
Perhaps this may change in the future.

The Scientist

The little animals may become the vectors of novel productivity, the bearers of a new wave of industrial riches, the solution to some environmental problems. Unlike pigs, insects can fly already: proof is gathering fast for a promising, yet realistic scenario.

(1) Studies of insects' eye function provide ideal models for the development of vision in robotics; (2) Understanding neuronal circuits in their brains gives clues to the researchers of artificial intelligence; (3) In vitro culture of insects produces great quantities of rare pharmaceuticals and foodstuff; (4) Mutant insects are proving to be ideal, non-toxic insecticides.

These are some of the insect stories unfolding at present: Let's pursue them a little further.

I'm still reading when reception calls me.

"Jim, it's Ros. I have a Dr John Harvey here for you."

"OK, I'll come downstairs." I didn't expect him to call on me and the meeting is not until 12.30 anyway, but I guess he wants to talk.

I fetch him and take him to the tenth floor, where we sit around the atrium. He has already apologised in the lift, saying he's early because he didn't know how long it would take from the airport in a taxi.

"Not to worry," I say, "we can get better acquainted."

"You may have noticed I'm not a very sociable person." He looks peculiarly vulnerable and at the same time sounds peremptory.

"OK, I'll tell you what's going to happen. I was able to glance at the meeting agenda." I hope this will relax him, but hit the wrong button.

"You've got a mole in there?" he asks quite aggressively.

"So you want to know or not?" This guy irritates me.

"Go ahead."

"Ok, the first item is an opening talk by Dr Gruber, who will explain how she'll conduct the meeting, and at that point she'll distribute the agenda."

"Why couldn't we have the agenda beforehand?"

"I guess she doesn't want to run the risk of having her plan for the meeting modified." I feel uneasy as I say this.

"What's next?" he asks curtly.

"You are next. You'll talk about your project. Yours is the main item, all the rest is discussion." I avoid the term criticism as John doesn't seem to expect any.

"What's the role of the research director, Lyanne?" he asks.

"She'll follow your project in between meetings. She'll give you a compliance sheet and she'll check where you are with that—very often." I don't repeat what Debbie told me about Lyanne: more ambitious than she appears to be.

"And Dr Gruber, what experience has she got in running an R&D company?"

He's obviously not read the many popular articles they wrote on her.

"This is her third," I say.

"And what happened to the other two?" He's instinctively critical. I should watch my back when my time comes.

"They were taken over. I heard she is determined to last longer this time." I'm saying too much.

Fortunately, Leon Kelly joins us and starts a jocular conversation.

"It's Canberra versus Sydney today, eh?" he says to John.

"Yes, and you could play in the scrum with your size."

"And you could play as the ball with your shape." Leon's tone is mild, even as he delivers a punch.

Carol is the last one to join us and arrives just seconds before Debbie comes and takes us inside.

Alba and Lyanne are already sitting at the table with a lot of papers before them. Alba gathers her stuff and gets up.

"Welcome to CoDis' first meeting. I look forward to a good discussion." She shows us the sandwiches arranged on a side table with orange juice, coffee and tea.

"Please help yourselves and take your place. We'll have a working lunch."

She sits again. She's wearing a summer dress that leaves exposed the joint of her arm with the shoulder. The angle forms a gracious shape that I hadn't noticed in a woman before.

"Jim, you are not going to eat?" Debbie offers me a plate.

There are a few minutes of respite, the first few bites at the sandwiches, and Alba starts with a smile.

"Welcome again. I'd like to tell you what are the qualities I like in a meeting: first, courtesy in addressing the others; then specificity when criticising their work; most of all, a problem-solving focus and a joint-venture spirit. Would you want to add others?"

"Yes," says Leon, "we should have fun. Being too serious spoils a good meeting."

"Granted, Leon." Alba smiles.

"OK," she continues while distributing papers, "here's the agenda. I trust every topic of interest is covered. But you may want to discuss something else under the item 'other'." She looks around and everyone nods.

"When we are more advanced in the projects, I'll ask you to circulate your reports before the meetings. But today we'll just hear what John has to tell us."

John has prepared some facts and figures, geographical maps and pictures, which are distributed around the table. Then he starts talking. Initially it's a longish lecture on insects, their classification, their numbers and distribution, all in the context of the great collections that the CSIRO has been able to put together over seven decades.

Next he talks of the specialties, the specific disciplines entomologists concentrate on, including his own: insect chemistry. He also says that our project will involve insect genetics to a certain extent, because that will determine more closely the species that will be found and used.

All in all, John establishes himself as a very clear thinking scientist, thoroughly competent and knowledgeable, if perhaps a little too sure of himself for my liking.

Alba seems satisfied. "Very good, John. That was very helpful. Now will you tell us something specific about the project?"

"I'll tell you first about the difficulties in starting our searches for insect species that may provide new antibiotics. One is permits. As we explore the tropical areas of the Northern Territory and Far North Queensland, we are inevitably confronted by the rights of the traditional owners."

We look at each other and at Alba. Everyone is clearly taken by surprise.

"Right," says John. "I knew you wouldn't have expected this; a big hurdle at the very beginning of the project." He seems strangely satisfied.

"How do you plan to overcome this?" Alba tries to keep her cool.

"We've been in talks with elders since October last year."

"I mean are you sure you need their permit?" Alba asks.

"Oh yes. Bioprospecting has been regulated for quite some time, mainly because of medicinal plants. Aborigines are used to directing new bioprospectors towards plants they have used for millennia. With insects this is less well established, but they consider the case to be exactly the same. And we will need them anyway, because their knowledge of where to find new insect species will help us immensely."

"OK, what is your plan then for acquiring their permits?" Alba pursues.

"We are drafting the agreements, but are stuck at the point of discussing the royalty rate on all future revenues. Here we need guidance from you." He's entered Alba's territory.

"Well," she says, "ours is a 50/50 joint venture. It's easy to envisage a situation where each of our 50% is going to be reduced by agreements with external players.

"I think it very reasonable that CoDis will have to reduce its share in future profits by dealing with the antibiotic company that will take our product to the market if we are successful.

"Equally, Entomology may need to reduce its share in favour of the original owners of the land where insects will be found." Alba seems quick to rationalise.

"You are saying that it's up to us to deal with the Aborigines and up to you to deal with the pharmaceutical industry," John concludes.

"Exactly," says Alba, "and CSIRO, I'm sure, can negotiate that directly with the elders."

"Ok, I'll talk with my Chief." John sits proudly on his chair.

"Any other hurdle?" Alba is slightly on edge.

"Just the usual delay in the delivery of the robotic system that is meant to analyze the many hundreds of chemicals we'll collect from new insects."

"And when do you expect delivery?" Alba's jaws twitch.

"Any time now: we had decided to order from the US a specific configuration of the equipment that is rather different from standard. In hindsight, we should have got the standard system delivered and change it here. But it's too late now."

"OK," says Alba, "any discussion?"

Carol and Leon, in turn, ask technical questions and John replies extensively. Lyanne interjects whenever she finds a pause in the others' discussion and reveals herself to be the real devil's advocate.

"How will you know, John," she asks, "that a compound you'll work on for months—culturing millions of insects, extracting and purifying it to a single molecule—is not one that someone else has already discovered in secret?"

"Well, Lyanne, we'll do all that work in secret ourselves and when we are ready, we'll rush in a patent application and a quick letter to *Nature* to announce the discovery. That goes on all the time in chemistry." He looks sort of triumphant.

"John, I was wondering." I take my time in formulating a new idea that developed in my mind while I was listening to them. "Among the many hundreds of new compounds that your robotics will eventually analyze, do you think there may be some that have a neurotoxic or neurorelaxing activity?"

"It could be, but I need to know what type of compounds you are thinking of." John is clearly not prepared to concede.

"But that's a great idea, Jim." Alba is excited. "We may end up with new drugs that we didn't even aim for at the beginning!" She turns her look around the table:

"You see, that's exactly the kind of thing I expected from our discussions together. When I dreamed up our management system, I could see people from different disciplines, looking from different angles, coming up with truly original ideas. An entomologist and a neuroscientist working together, isn't that fantastic?"

While Alba keeps talking, I see myself in the form of a Janus-like double face (did He have one brain and two faces or also two brains?). One face looks at Harvey. I have stopped him in his tracks; at least I've ended his dominance around the table by offering him a novel path to our discoveries. The other face is turned towards Alba, beginning to make her happy with the same brilliant idea. I get satisfaction on both counts, glad to win my tiny battles, and send a quick, tender look over to her while hiding my glee from Harvey. But I feel a sudden change in my mood when I think of these two fighters: their want for winning is so raw, while defeat is still possible, that a wave of anxiety surges in my mind and spoils the play.

***

Eight

5 November 2015. Lunch in the garden by the pool. Martina is home for a change and wants to relax, being very tired most of the time. I'm happy to prepare the meal and serve it to her down here.

I have cooked a prawn risotto and serve it with a fennel, tomato and basil salad. I've even baked some pinoli biscotti to dip in the *Vin Santo* that Angiolino gave me on his return from Tuscany last October.

Martina had a swim and is now in the shower that used to be Max's when he lived down here in the room at pool level. Sometimes I use that space for an afternoon nap after a long morning spent writing in the garden.

All refreshed, Martina is glowing and smiles, seeing the food on the table: "That's my favorite risotto, Jim!"

Perhaps because we don't get together very often these days, we seem to be kinder to each other. My trips to Paris are less frequent and my job as a science journalist has been only part-time since I started writing the book. In the opposite direction, Martina is busier and busier, living practically an independent life.

"You know that I've never understood your bent for cooking? What is it about, food and you?"

Her question is new and strange. She's always preferred to rely on her sharp eye than to probe my mind more deeply. So her attention has been focused on those superficial signs of my emotions that, without my wanting, are the open book she can read readily. But my elaborated feelings, those more deeply ingrained sentiments that were invisible to her, she didn't want to know. She must have decided that her legalistic need-to-know-basis stopped at the superficial level, at the outwardly visible, especially at the unintentionally expressed signs of my emotions. She never bothered with my feelings, those that are a stable part of my consciousness and that form an important part of my mind. Until now, it seems.

"How long have you got? I could keep you stuck on the subject for hours."

"Just a few hints will do."

"OK. One: cooking food changed the anatomy of digestion and the evolution of modern man took flight from there. I think it's the single most important cultural change of mankind in evolutionary terms."

"More important than sex?"

"Sex is nothing special in the animal kingdom: a good way to mix and spread genes? Yes, but that doesn't give a particular evolutionary advantage to man. Sexual pleasure is an old evolutionary trick to get reproduction."

"What else?"

"The smell of food activates our olfactory neurons and can be a potent vehicle for memory; it's such a powerful recall that it could be used in therapy."

"One last reason?" Martina is not hooked by any of this, it's clear.

"This is very personal and you might not agree, but cooking food is, for me, the only physical activity in which I see the possibility of elegance: ingeniously simple and pleasing."

"How's the book coming along?" She asks too many questions today. What's up?

"Well, I think I'm on chapter eight. But only the first draft."

"What's the mood at the moment?" She is familiar with my story.

"Still pretty buoyant: at the beginning of the projects when we were all enthusiastic, hopeful, and totally unaware of the fraudsters' dealings."

"When did they start their manoeuvres?"

"From the very beginning of our venture. I heard the story much later, but apparently they used to meet once a month in Northbridge at a sort of investment club. There were some twenty men going regularly and discussing the share market, stocks supposed to go up or down. The leader was a man who had bought shares in CoDis at the very beginning, by the name of Nolan. He was apparently the mastermind."

"I thought Joel Patricks was that," she says.

"At the time I thought that too. But apparently Patricks only provided an example, a precedent that he used in Western Australia at the time of Poseidon. Then, he got off scot-free but had to move out of town, his reputation in tatters. Unfortunately our chairman didn't know that. But Nolan did, took him on board and updated the scheme to suit the specific needs of their plot."

"But were all twenty involved?" Martina can't believe that.

"No, no, the plotters were just those three, Patricks, Nolan and Cooper. The others were unwitting victims of the manipulation."

"In what way?"

"Five months after the share issue, when we were just adjusting to our new projects, the trio started talking the company down to depress the share price. Remember that two of them were Directors on CoDis Board, so supposedly in the know of privileged information. But they were shrewd, and Cooper was a lawyer.

"They started appearing just disappointed and depressed, sending out negative vibes about the Company. Then Nolan hinted that he was going to sell part of his stock and others followed."

"But how do you know all this?" Martina is baffled.

"Word of one to another; Alba told me that Paul Creagan had a friend of a friend in the club." I remember well Alba's anger at that.

"Then what happened?"

"Of course the share price dropped once the word got out that people close to Directors on the Board were selling. By June 1997 it reached a low of fifty cents, half the issue price."

"And what did Alba and the Chair do?"

"There was little they could do. It was too early for positive results so announcements were out of the question; there was little turnover of shares and even the few sellers had to reduce their asking price. At the same time, there was also the beginning of the Asian financial crisis and the markets in Australia were generally depressed."

"And the plotters?"

"They were totally inconspicuous for several months. Then in about November that year, Alba and Paul started hearing of some buying by obscure stockbrokers in Western Australia. The share register now included nominee companies that gave their address in various parts of the world including, as you know, Turkey, because they didn't want to reveal that they were associated."

"Yes, I know the story from here. What a shambles!" Martina seems determined to change the subject. "And Alba? I've never known when you two started."

"At around that very time, when her confidence in the plan was shaken by those events."

I am not sure why Martina wants to talk about this.

"It's been such a long time," Martina says. "It doesn't hurt anymore if you talk about it."

"Well, I'm not at liberty to do that," I state firmly.

"Why?" Martina seems genuinely surprised.

Still, that annoys me. "Would you ask me the same question if it were one of your client-lawyer relationship? Why do you take your privilege of confidentiality above ours. Why do you discount the importance of a pact between us to keep things private, as she wanted?"

"Ok, ok, we could argue about that, but she didn't need to make such a fuss.

After all, affairs are not that unusual." Again Martina displays a very matter-of-fact attitude.

"Possibly."

"You must have had quite a conflictual relationship." Martina is always so predictable in her comments.

"Not at all. I understood her problem and that was enough for us."
That sense of contentment grips me still.

"Strange that you didn't consider leaving with her."

"She never asked me to. From the beginning she said very firmly
that she would never forgive herself for breaking up a marriage."

"Would you have done it if she wanted you to?" Martina is now
quite serious. It would be better to say no.

"Yes, I think I would have. I'm sorry, but you said yourself that I
was in a state of confusion then."

"Did she say goodbye before leaving Australia?"

"Not really, but I remember very well what she said the last time
we spoke:

'You know, when I think of my romantic life, thirty-odd years, I
guess I've been lucky to have found men who made me generally happy.
Then there is you. You made me so perfectly content that I want you to
stay in my mind as the finest and last love.'"

"That's serious stuff." Martina leaves the table, then she turns and
asks: "When are you due back in Paris next?"

"In two weeks time."

"Right."

*

Two weeks later, as I was preparing to leave once more for Paris, my
wife, uncharacteristically in a bad temper, made a startling comment:
"Just as well; you're never here anyway, even when your body is."

Was my body useless; was this the subtext of her comment? "Why
do you say that?" I'm surprised.

"Your mind, where is it? Always somewhere else!"

"But I do what you want me to do, don't I? And I've done that for
ages."

"Of course, of course. Don't start telling me that you have been
picking up the kids from school for decades, put food on their table and

so on. I know all that. But your mind was always elsewhere and they knew it."

"They rarely engaged me in any sort of conversation; they treated me like a supply manager, while with you they were tender, joking and free-wheeling."

"I knew what they wanted to talk about. I met their friends, I took them to fun holidays, remember?"

"Yes, and all that in the minimum time possible and under your strict schedules. You've always been a great manager of your time as well as of your love for them!"

Is it normal for a man to publicize to his children how much they mean to him? Wasn't it obvious by the way I took care of them, by being always available?

"Well," Martina raised her voice to be heard, "do you think our marriage is doing fine?"

"Yes, of course."

"In what way?"

"As us being together and caring for each other. As our story developing without major frictions, four people who have managed to build a precious, unique life together."

"And do you think that's enough?"

"I do and would like that to go on for at least another generation."

"Jim, I've found a man who's helping me to relax and have fun: he's a colleague without fancy intellectual ambitions who understands perfectly what I'm about. We're going to live together, in his City apartment during the week and in his Palm Beach house on weekends."

A distinct, pointed pain hit me in the chest; for a few seconds I could see only vague forms in front of me and yet, in a calm voice I'm still proud of, I said softly: "If that's what you want . . . Max and Joan . . . do they know?"

"Of course. They've seen Kevin a few times and like him. But he doesn't mean much to them, now they're adult and independent. By the way, do you think you'll keep this big house?" She never liked that responsibility.

"Probably . . . You know, my father wouldn't have liked me to sell his estate. Joan and Max can still come here to stay whenever they like."

Moving to her desk, Martina took from it the divorce papers ready to be signed before I left. An easy task from a patrimonial point of view, since we had separate assets: she was keeping the bonds I gave her regularly on our anniversaries, the jewels and the car. With her law partnership, a well-endowed superannuation scheme and a new provider, she didn't do badly. She also had a 30-year history with four lives in it: a massive sequence of memories that would stay undivided in her mind.

What will she do with those undivided memories? Will they survive brightly or take second place in her mind to the novelty of the fun she'll experience from now on? Did she ever care for that sense of family that is also identity, the individuality of a group that has shared decades of life together? I know only that I'll want to remember always the four of us together, our normal life that, looked at from within and attentively, had a precious and unique identity with the character of our mix, the rhythm of our exchanges and the strings of our mutual affection.

***

Nine

3-9 March 1997. "It doesn't make sense."

Alba has summoned me to her office and is talking about the fall in the share price, a highly unusual trend as far as she is concerned.

"You see, Jim, the investors who subscribed our share issue would have known that for the first few years they needed to be patient. Why would they sell now? It doesn't make sense."

"Well, it's a fact though. What are you going to do about it?" I ask.

"Yes, that's the reason I called you." She sits at the table where several pages are scattered in apparent disorder. Debbie brings us coffee and then gathers the pages, looking at their numbers. She smiles at me with an intended message I don't understand.

"I was angry a minute ago," Alba says, aware of that exchange, "but you may be my solution, Jim."

"Yes?" I have no clue as to what she's going to ask me.

"The idea is to try to counteract the share price fall with a newspaper article by Glennys Bell."

"She's written about you several times, I think."

"That's right, and she's willing to do it again, this time on one of our projects."

"But we have no results yet."

"Yes, but an article on the opportunities of our projects—one by Glennys Bell, who has a great writing style but also a visually poetic streak—may remind the public of the worth of our work."

"Sure, and did you want to have it on my project?"

"Actually, no. This morning I received Carol's report on her project and thought that it could be the right subject for an article. Then of course I realised that her account was so technical, poor Glennys wouldn't be able to dig into it."

"We can translate it, of course."

"Exactly, and that's where you come into the picture."

"Wouldn't Lyanne be able to do it?"

"Oh no. With her metric mind, she can measure progress or the lack of it, she can note delays and assign man/hours, but she has no appreciation of the value of things. Her horizon is a sequence of numbers; I want blue sky."

"And you see blue in my mind." I can't help smiling.

"Definitely."

"Ok, I'll try." I'm not sure I'm flattered as a scientist, but I like it.

"To be sure, can you check your interpretation with Carol, just in case?" she adds.

"Of course. And when is the article due?"

"Glennys has a space in her magazine on the 9th of March." Alba looks satisfied.

"But that's the day of our management meeting!"

"Indeed! That's why we need a realistic/blue-sky article." Alba laughs.

"At least admit that you've given me a near impossible task."

"I admit that I'm testing you, yes."

*

In a couple of days I go over the basics of the topic Carol is specialised in. It is a completely different field from mine, but fortunately it has plenty of publications I can consult, papers that Carol has given me. I decide that for Glennys, it's important to have a broad view, rather than specific technical detail.

Carol agrees and gives me her go ahead. So I write a brief article that stretches my ability to put in layman's language a complex scientific project.

Prevention of Malignant Changes

The function of the immune system is well known; it fights foreign entities like bugs or transplanted organs. What is less known is a particular traffic of immune cells and molecules in mucosal sites like the gut and the lung. This type of selected traffic constitutes the mucosal (or secretory) immune system.

The two, peripheral blood and mucosal systems, have not only a different geography but also a different mix of immune components. To the point that looking for some immune cells in the blood will give a very different picture from that of the gut mucosa. Naturally, local immune reactions depend on the local traffic and on its components.

In the gut, it is relatively common to find inflammation of the mucosa, which is an abnormally high immune reaction that may give rise to the so-called inflammatory bowel disease (IBD). This can be chronic or acute and forms a range of pathologies. Often IBD turns to cancer, a much more serious disease. This change may be due to a number of factors, from inflammation suppressors to genetic mutations or breakdown of the DNA repair system.

This project intends to observe, over a period of three years, these changes in patients with IBD or colon cancer. Why? We want to pick up the differences between those patients with IBD who progress to cancer from those who do not.

There are various ways to study this. (Here I went on giving some of the details, that Glennys may wish to know anyway, about the mechanics of the study, then concluded.)

All these reactions, all these cells and factors participating to immune activities, and perhaps to neoplastic change, need to be observed in real time. We want to monitor them over three years and see if they can give us a clear picture of what happens. In this way, we may be able to construct a model of prevention, a way in which certain changes can be stopped by medical intervention and normality preserved.

What do we need to do to prevent IBD from turning to cancer? At the end of this project we hope to be able to tell you.

*

"It's a pale shade of blue, Jim," Alba says when she reads it, but looks satisfied and sends it to Glennys Bell. Alba is so convinced it will work that she hasn't even asked the Chairman for his opinion. But Paul Creagan is angry when he reads about it. I happen to be in her office when he rushes in.

"That was a silly move, Alba. I expected you to understand these things. We will appear defensive, as if we needed help from a magazine that has glorified you in the past and it's only too ready to give you a hand now. From **today**, you'll check with me every single move that may have an impact on share price. Understood?"

Alba has her head down, as if looking at her shoes, and nods. She doesn't say anything, so I move to leave. But Paul stops me.

"Jim, we need to face the fact that the share price will fall further. It doesn't really matter at this stage, except that we are a good takeover target. With the money we've got and the interest we are earning, our shares are currently priced at half the Company's net asset value in cash."

I don't understand why he is telling me this.

"What I'm saying, Jim, is that you and the other three project leaders have to try really hard to have quick results so that we can make some announcement soon and lift the share price."

"That wasn't the agreement! Of course we want to have results, but I thought we had three years and it's only been five months!"

"Of course, of course." Paul's tone is mild with me, down from the irritated voice he used with Alba. "I'm just trying to explain the unexpected. There is clearly a game out there that some people are playing with us. I just want you to know that we've been taken by surprise and that your projects have no longer the leisure time we thought you could have."

I look at him and feel rattled.

"What Paul is saying, Jim," Alba's voice is forced and unnatural, "is that things may change if the Company is taken over."

"What do you mean?" I ask.

"She means," Paul replies before Alba, "that speculators are interested only in our cash, not our projects. They would terminate the joint ventures straight after their takeover."

"But we have a legal agreement for three-year funding!" In a flash I think of our new staff, of our commitment to them.

"The new owners would find a way to get out of it. You see, if they invest our cash in another business, you would have no prospect of recouping your funds from them."

"Jim, I'll see you at the management meeting this afternoon. Now I need to talk with Paul." Alba's tone is almost robotic, her face tense, and as she sits down with him, I notice her hand shaking.

*

The management meeting starts as usual, except that Alba is late and Debbie whispers in my ear: "Alba wants you to explain to the others what the Chairman told you this morning." So I tell them.

Carol is the first to comment when I'm finished: "I knew it, Jim. I shouldn't have agreed to this."

Leon takes a more positive view: "What I think we should do is to talk our projects up whenever we can out there. So that we create some interest, and if this thing turns out badly, we may get alternative funding."

John comes up with the most realistic suggestion and starts talking just as Alba enters the room:

"Well, good afternoon to you. I'm glad you're here so I don't have to repeat myself." He takes a pause and looks around him as if to make sure everyone is listening. In fact, even Debbie is, while she pretends to attend to our lunch.

"Ok, I think my project can solve our problem. And this is why."

He explains that CSIRO has successfully signed the permits with traditional owners in the Northern Territory and Far North Queensland. The permits are exclusive, so Entomology is the only group with legal access to the insect populations there. Exclusive access, plus their group's know-how, plus the equipment now functioning; all this is a commodity that the whole specialised world of bioprospecting would value.

"We could find a partner in the pharmaceutical industry willing to pay millions upfront for the privileged access to all that!"

We look at Alba, her eyes vacuously fixed on John.

"Yes," she says after a while, her face still concentrating, but clearly not on his person, "it's a good, desperate move." She turns her face towards the centre of the table and seems recomposed. "I think we should keep it as a last resort."

She smiles at John. "Thank you, it's very generous of you to offer this to us. Of course you understand that any agreement of this kind would be with CoDis, therefore any revenue from that would increase our cash and its desirability as a takeover target."

She takes another pause, then continues: "But if an announcement of that kind moved the share price upward substantially, then things would change. It would all depend on good timing. Thank you again, John, I'll talk with Paul about it."

She turns to the agenda of the meeting and asks Carol to talk about her project.

Carol is stiff and inhibited. She presents her project as if distancing from it. But Alba doesn't allow her to finish too quickly.

"Tell us, Carol, how do you obtain specimens for testing immune cells and cytokines at mucosal level?"

"Our Uni is associated with the Hospital, as you know. Well, we have a tacit agreement with the gastroenterologists there and we can get specimens from them at any time. You see, they participate to our research projects and get their names on the papers we publish." Carol seems to have warmed up again to the project and is now willing to elaborate:

"All patients who undergo endoscopies or colonoscopies will provide, without further procedures, their specimens. One of our technicians goes there and waits outside until a nurse comes out and delivers a vial that contains liquid from the mucosal washings. These contain immune cells and cytokines.

"In this way, we get hold of about fifteen to twenty specimens a week, together with the medical history of the coded patients."

We continue to talk about Carol's project, asking technical questions. John asks the most critical ones. He clearly has a very analytical mind. But his tone seems to have suddenly mellowed.

"Your project, Carol, is to find out what are the markers of a potential progression from bowel inflammation to cancer. Will you look for these markers in immune cells only, or in any other cells?"

"Good point, John. Initially we will look for markers in immune cells or in their products, the cytokines. If we can't find in them any correlation with cancer, then we'll look at other cells."

My questions are more Dorothy Dixers whose answers I know, except that they'll put Carol's project in much more favourable light:

"So, calculating a minimum of 100 weeks in three years, you'll get between 1500 and 2000 specimens. If everything goes well, and you are clear on your preventative action, how many patients can avoid getting a cancer?"

Carol smiles as she replies, knowing exactly what I am doing:

"Even a 3% result, which is at the very low end, would benefit forty five to sixty people, just in our hospital."

Leon doesn't pose questions, but shares his reflections:

"I think this meeting has been very important, Alba. It has cemented our collaboration against the dangers out there and I think we are thoroughly united in that. More significantly, though, it has strengthened our conviction that what we are doing here is for the benefit and health of many patients, not for the interest or greed of some Bourse Brigands!"

That's the first time we hear that term and laugh, Alba included.

But the mood around the table is subdued and an embarrassed silence follows before people get up without waiting for Alba's formal words to close the meeting.

Leon pats her gently on the shoulder before leaving to catch a plane for Canberra. Harvey follows suit—he is catching the same plane—but not before declaring proudly: "We'll fight this battle together."

Carol gives Alba a long hug and whispers something in her ear. This, more than anything else, signals the softening of Alba's position, solidarity replacing the awe of her leadership that everyone felt until now.

I pretend to leave and walk around the largely empty and dimly lit 10th floor, while keeping an eye on CoDis' quarters through its glass front. Debbie is the last to leave. Soon after, Alba walks out of her office and approaches the wall in the entrance where the Company's logo is affixed. There is a solid, dark blue, large C with its lower end-bit lifted to expose a yellow underside. The lifted corner reveals a little red D that has its top tilted backwards in apparent response to an accelerated advance. Cooperation and discovery are linked there to good effect.

With her left hand, Alba touches the logo in a circular movement over the C as if to mimic writing it, then moves her right hand closer to the D and holds it in perspective between her forefinger and thumb. She stays there for a while, her eyes fixed on the logo. I come out of hiding and wave my arms, careful to flag my presence to her, until she sees me and smiles. Then I pirouette my approach. She laughs and comes to the door. I get closer as she opens, bow, then raise my head:

"Ma'am wishes to play?"

"Oh yes!"

***

Ten

7 April 1997. There will be confluence.

Our management meeting is going to merge with the Board of Directors' meeting. It is really an extraordinary gathering that is meant to give Board members the chance to ask questions of the scientists. Science being the Company's business, they would want to know more after six months of operations. So said the Chairman.

Given the large number, Rob has volunteered the Institute's boardroom and Denyse has organised a sophisticated lunch based on sandwiches as usual, but of higher quality. As for their motivations, Rob is there as host and clearly wants to be close to the discussion, so that he'll be able to take immediate stock of the situation. For her part, I'm sure Denyse wants to show us the different class she belongs to, that of administration.

When we enter the large room, we can't fail to notice a three-meter long mural installation, a composition of bright blue *papier-machè* pieces that gives a strange sense of movement and action.

"It's by Janet Laurence," says Rob. "I asked her last year to study biological specimens under the microscope, cells and chromosomes: to look at graphs showing the mechanisms of cell reproduction, at pictures of DNA's structure and so on. She then projected in her mind the sense of activity that goes on down there in the microscopic world and was able to express it in this composition. It's called Meyosis."

I've seen it before, so I can concentrate on the impression this work of art makes on some of the people present here.

Leon laughs quietly. I ask him why he find it amusing.

"It's sex, clearly. She has represented sexual elements."

Carol looks at him contemptuously. "I find it amazing, Leon, that you can still laugh at this. Of course what she wanted to depict is the very split of sexual elements from cellular chromosomes."

Roth Cooper seems rather disgusted: "It could be construed as obscene," he says, while Joel Patricks spits a bit of sandwich as he opens his mouth: "I'm glad we didn't pay for this."

The Director/computer expert goes to the farthest point of observation in the room before venturing: "Of course this artist has great command of abstract symbols and a sure hand when it comes to depict action."

The Chairman invites us to sit down as soon as Alba enters the room. She takes a glass of water and chooses a place on his right. Lyanne is on his left, ready with a large minute book and a long blank pad in front of her. I didn't know she was also the Company Secretary.

"Thank you for coming here today," Paul says. "This is a unique opportunity to canvas questions and ideas in the most frank way possible. We are not deterred by the falling share price, for which someone must be responsible, even perhaps a couple of people around this table." He pauses and looks at Cooper and Patricks.

"What's important here is not the problem, but the solution. Let's start with asking Professor Latimar to tell us if her project has a chance of giving early results."

"Frankly, no, it's not possible." Carol's voice reflects clearly her irritation. "We have stated several times that we need the full three years."

"Can you tell us why?" Paul looks as if he knows and exchanges a nod with Alba. At that point she is sipping some water and her hand is shaking again.

"We need to study," says Carol, "at least 1500 specimens. That seems a lot of patients, but then we have to split them by pathology. Some will have ulcerative colitis, others Crohns' Disease—both are inflammatory bowel diseases—while others will have cancer. So if you start dividing 1500 by 3, you'll have 500 in each group. Split them again by sex, and then by two age groups, and you'll have only 125 in each category, the very minimum for a statistically significant outcome."

"Ok, thank you, Professor." Paul turns to Leon:

"What about you, Professor Kelly?" He has changed tone slightly: less paternalistic than with Carol, more aggressive with Leon.

"Oh, Mr. Chairman, you know," Leon shakes his head with the hint of a smile, "we are dealing with children here."

"You said in the Prospectus," Cooper raises his voice in apparent affront, "that you will be using a product that has already been approved by health authorities in Australia!"

"You are right. I did, and that's true; what we want to use is an approved product. But, as I said, we deal with children. Before we can test our hypothesis—which, by the way, seems proven in animal models that we have tested in the last six months—before that we will have to run a controlled clinical trial in children as young as seven."

"Why?" Paul now seems alarmed.

"Because the Q-fever vaccine—the one we want to use to disrupt the autoimmune reaction that is destroying their pancreas, and that will give them diabetes if we don't intervene—that vaccine has only been used in adults and strong, healthy farmhands at that. We need to recruit 150 children who have signs of incipient diabetes and test on them several safe doses of that vaccine."

Under his amiability, Leon can't hide his contempt for these people who put questions of time and money before such an important health issue.

"Ok, two down," says Cooper.

"If there is anything down here," the Chairman looks at Cooper and seems to have picked up where Leon left, "it is your probable involvement in depressing our share price and rendering a worthy project so difficult to carry out."

"I believe it's my turn," I say.

"Yes. Go ahead, Jim." Paul's face is still red with anger.

"Well, I'm afraid my case aligns with the other two. In the past six months we have been able to adjust our program for the confocal microscopy to the study of olfactory neurons."

"Has your programmer solved the algorithm problem?" The computer expert/director asks about some advice he gave us in the past month or so.

"Yes, it all works well now and we have started to collect comparative data from the confocal microscope, so that in the end people will be able to stain the neurons just using an optical microscope to identify diverse structures in different neurological conditions. But, we need precise data to be sure."

"What is your limiting factor?" The physicist/director is sitting very straight and asks the question with an air of authority that must come from usually fronting people in need of her bank.

"Recruitment, by far. We can collect biopsies only from people who are suspected to have a neurodegenerative condition. It could be old people with Alzheimer's or young adults with a drug problem. Difficult people to deal with."

"Well, I must say," Patricks still has some crumbs of biscuit on one corner of his thin mouth, "I thought biotech research was like mineral exploration. You went for a lode of gold or copper, and you found it or not."

"Mr Patricks," Rob intervenes, "let me tell you the difference; here the lode is not one concentrated treasure of gold or copper. It is widespread riches of knowledge. In biology, wherever you dig you find something: some way of understanding how millions of years of evolution have conserved a particular trick of communication among cells, a certain type of signal they use; or the mechanism whereby neurons try to compensate for trauma and adapt to a condition that may have threatened life. The riches are not just information, they are knowledge we can use to prevent disease or repair it. These riches are everywhere in biology, not in a chance hit."

Every one is silent, taking in what Rob has just said, until John, insensitive as ever, grabs our attention:

"Well, I think that leaves me and I'm glad I can announce that my project is ahead of schedule and that there is every chance that we'll be able to find a commercial partner soon."

"How do you plan to go about it, John?" Paul is all ears.

"In June there will be an international conference: it is a biennial meeting on Bioprospecting. It will be held in San Diego, California, and all major players will be there. I intend to go."

"Alba, what do you think?" Paul seems to know the answer: "You said you wanted to wait for the right opportunity."

"Yes, I agree with John," Alba says in a calm voice. "We should go. If he presents a paper on insects, I can talk with various industry participants. The two of us should be able to put up a double act that would at least explore in full, and in one go, the opportunity that John has described."

I feel a pang of envy. Is it for the easy task John has got with his 'bugs and chemistry' project versus the difficulties of our medical ones? Or is it because of the company he'll keep in America, away from the obnoxious manoeuvres down here?

***

Eleven

2 October 1997. Today is the first anniversary of CoDis' listing on the Australian Stock Exchange. At lunch Alba joined Paul and some institutional investors for a quiet celebration in town. On her return, she called me, asking if I would join her for drinks with Debbie on the 10th floor. It would be after work at about 6 pm. She is in an expansive mood. We are sitting in the hall of her office, on the lounge CoDis bought at considerable expense.

"It was a great choice," she says. "You can feel with your fingertips the beautiful material, part natural fiber, part mysterious new invention, all made in your ancestors' country."

"Yes," I'm happy to say, "my father told me that in the financial crisis of the 70s, many Italian architects went into furniture design for lack of other, more monumental work."

Debbie brings out the drinks: Campari soda for Alba, gin and tonic for me, and beer for herself. She's prepared grissini with prosciutto crudo, green and black olives, plus a tranche of a Parmesan wheel that has a knife with a round, but pointed blade impaled in it. Alba flicks the knife and a small, irregular piece of cheese falls into her hand.

"It's so fresh when cut this way!"

It's good to see her in this light mood. In the past six months she has practically withdrawn from view, with the only exception of management meetings, and left to Paul all public tasks, including shareholders and media relations.

"You know," she giggles, "I can't stop laughing when I think of that day in June, just before we left for the US. Did I ever tell you what happened?"

"No, and I didn't think you'd be laughing then."

"I was desperate! The share price was at its lowest. I didn't want to leave and told Paul that much."

"Had you changed your mind?" I ask. "You had agreed to the trip."

"Yes, but I had the impression of abandoning ship." Alba shakes her head with a half smile and continues. "Of course Paul would have nothing of it. He said:

'Listen, Alba, this is a good chance to test our opportunity for an important strategic alliance. And time presses. You mightn't get another chance and your very creature might drop in the hands of unscrupulous people.'

"So what is there to laugh about?" I ask while picking an olive.

"It was Harvey. He was there with us, several inches shorter than me, and he was saying:

'Paul, trust me. I'll take her to the US, even if I have to carry her myself!'

She continues to laugh, takes off her jacket and muscles up her silky, long arms.

"But it was a good trip, wasn't it?" Debbie is determined to be part of the conversation.

"Sure. We did exactly what we needed to do and got a good result, as everybody now knows." She drinks and starts laughing again. I suspect Debbie put too much Campari and little soda in her glass.

"You know, I have this other image in my mind of Harvey the entomologist entering a conference room in San Diego, looking around, seeing me and immediately changing course, exactly like an insect."

"So you didn't talk at all?" Debbie is curious about human behaviour, especially when it diverts from normal expectations.

"We did, but only when I invited him for dinner."

I know that they both stayed at the Hotel Del Coronado, an institution in San Diego that was refurbished in 1920 for the visit of the future King of England, Edward VIII.

"So did you have dinner at the Hotel?" I ask.

"No, no. I chose a small restaurant near the boardwalk in San Diego, the right place to have clam chowder."

"And?" Debbie is curiously waiting to hear what happened there.

"Nothing much. I made an enormous effort to try and extract information from him and get him to talk about the people who had expressed interest in his work, in particular the French group I'm negotiating with now."

"By the way, how is it going?" An important question, I think.

"It's going well. But of course the French are slow in the negotiations. They will come to visit Sydney and Canberra next month. Then, if they are satisfied, we'll have to go to Castres, their headquarters in France."

"Can you speak French?" I ask, still knowing so little about her.

"Yes, my parents came from Alsace, so as a child I learnt both German and French before starting on English at school."

I am surprised to hear her talking this way; she's been so secretive about her families, past and present, until now.

"So you won't need my help. Pity."

She smiles but her expression is suddenly sad.

"And now? What's happening to the share price?" Debbie takes her, perhaps deliberately, to an alternative-thinking platform.

"Today it was at 95 cents, almost par value," Alba responds automatically, "but of course many things are happening."

'What do you mean?" I join them on the platform.

"The situation is tricky. On the one hand there are buyers who may have heard about the deal with the French, though that information should be restricted to the Directors on the Board."

"Who is buying? Can you trace them from the share register?" I ask, having learnt about the existence of that register only last night over dinner with my father.

"Yes, up to a point. There are many nominees that we don't know. We have started to investigate where they come from." Alba is less sanguine than me on this and gives the impression that she would prefer not to know.

"You said that there are some Turkish people buying." Debbie insists.

"Yes, and you know, Paul has given the evidence to Trevor Sykes for an article in *The Australian Financial Review*."

"What sort of evidence?" I ask.

"They have traced a nominee company that has a woman from Instanbul as the Director. Trevor is going to do this article imagining her to be a belly dancer with an interest in Australian Biotech!"

I know from my father that Sykes writes under the pseudonym of PierPont and is very effective with his policing of companies, but also with his distinctive kind of sharp humour.

"Is there still a danger of takeover?"

"Definitely." She is quite serious now.

"So what is the Brigands' game?" I'm rather confused.

"Officially, they won't buy many more shares. But if their covert associates do, they can still accumulate, under the regulatory radar, an important block of shares that they control and use against us."

"But how?"

"They can use their cumulative voting power, say of 35 to 40%, to kick out the directors who oppose them, namely Paul and me."

"And then?" I'm getting flustered by all these manoeuvres.

"And then they take control of the whole company and can use our gold chest in whatever way they choose. And that won't go to charity or research, for sure."

Debbie starts packing up and moves back and forth from the tearoom, but Alba is still in an expansive mood, not ready to close. I detect an urge to talk, even a rush to break with her usual reserve, as if determined to cut down any possible misunderstanding about her.

"When I was a scientist, I felt a kind of rage at the lack of money. Money seemed, then, a mirage that would buy better and better equipment and hire more and more people. That is why I went into business. I renounced my own research but I thought I could get finance for other credible scientists like you.

"Now I've spent years on the margins of the money world and I can tell you I don't belong there. Of course I don't belong any more to your scientific world either: once out, one stays out. But I found that between science and money, there is an interface, a niche for me. In there, I can do what I really like to do: to pick a good scientific enterprise in its early stages and help to advance it to the next step; to push it up to the point of relay, to add value in the process so that someone else can pursue it further until it becomes beneficial."

I try to break her monologue, but doubt it will work: "It can't be easy."

"No, but it can be done. It has been done."

"And your sense of belonging? Where does it lie?" After all, I'd like to know.

"It lies in the transition, in a role that lasts longer than you imagine. Think of all the steps in a long process that starts from brushing up my knowledge to understand and pick a promising scientific project; to put it into a different format, not just in terms of language but also in terms of tasks, so that the business element is the one that appears on the face of it, even if the substance remains very much a scientific endeavor. To negotiate conditions that are equitable and acceptable to both sides; to bring to you scientists the folding stuff; to watch that you spend it wisely and in the right direction and to wait for you to produce the goods. Throughout all that I become part of your transient scientific enterprise. That's where I belong." Alba pauses as if considering her task completed. Now she turns to me: "And you? What do you really want from your work?"

"I want to pursue the truth."

"A small task."

"I'm not in a hurry: got a lifetime for that."

"Seriously, though, tell me more. I'm intrigued."

"Ok, you asked for it. Truth in science is an approximation, of course, not an absolute value. And it depends, like everything else, on the fourth dimension: time.

"In time, certain scientific ideas get closer and closer to the truth. Naturally you need to factor in all the subjective interpretations along the way: that's the democracy of science.

"But at a certain point, click, the truth over a certain point crystallizes and almost everyone agrees. In time, William Harvey's blood circulation theory prevailed; Charles Darwin's evolution still stands, even if some details don't; Galileo's revolution ended up being accepted even by the Catholic Church. That's knowledge integrated with experience over time becoming the truth."

Alba is listening still.

"But if you think of time, you can envisage a race: the one who gets closest to the truth first, wins. That's the standard reward in science: first to describe it, even first to think it. In my case, I don't so much run in the race as I observe others racing and like to anticipate (you may call that punting) who's going to win, or rather which theory is going to get to the truth first."

"Isn't that a little idle?"

"Not at all. Because if I trust my knack to anticipate the truth, I apply it to my work, often with very good practical results. Then I'll have integrated my punt ahead of time."

"And isn't your selection of the possible truth rather subjective?"

"Of course, but I still go on and test experimentally if it works in my own research project. If it does, and is confirmed independently at any later stage, my punt was right and the truth is on my side."

***

Twelve

May-July 1998. "Why would a Turkish lass have chosen an Australian minnow—of all the listed stock—for a three quarter of a million punt, Pierpont asks himself. A whisper from a rug trader in the bazaar? A tip from a belly dancer? Pierpont was so intrigued that he did a little research. This yielded interesting coincidences."

The quote was part of an article Trevor Sykes wrote on the subject of CoDis in this period. "The Turkish lass by the name of Ayse" is a director of an Istanbul company whose co-director, Don, based in Guernsey, is another far-flung investor to be seized by enthusiasm for the Australian biotech company. One of Don's companies holds 6.7% and the other 1.7% of CoDis.

"Wondering idly what other companies had Don as a director, PierPont did another ASIC search." He found one company that had a wine operation in Scone, NSW. Another director of that company was no other than Nolan, of the Sydney suburb of Northbridge. Nolan, of course, was yet another investor in CoDis, partly through a New Zealand vehicle. His family companies owned at least 4.5%. So with Ayse, the associated interests reached over 25%.

"It would be nice to think that investors as far apart as New Zealand, Guernsey, Turkey and Northbridge had clubbed together to buy a biotech stock as a gesture of support. Nice but inaccurate, because as soon as these characters bought their stock, they called an extraordinary general meeting to sack its Chairman and the Managing Director."

Sykes was the first to alert us of the illegal nature of their manoeuvre.

"What Nolan plans to do next is unknown, but PierPont assumes that he will want to make a takeover bid for the rest of the shares.

"Briefly, the Corporation Law requires a bid to be made whenever a party—alone or in association with others—acquires more than 20% of a company."

He went on to explain why the associated groups would be legally bound to make a bid for the rest of the shares at the top price they paid in the past.

"It would seem to me that Nolan could escape such a bid only if he succeeded in proving Ayse was not an associate. If that is so, PierPont would dearly love someone to explain Turkish investment strategies. In Ayse's case, it consisted in spending three quarters of a mill to buy 8% of a small company in a foreign country 10,000 miles away so she could vote to sack the chairman and the managing director. Something odd there, surely?"

When Alba showed me PierPont's article I had already heard about it. The Institute was buzzing with rumours and questions about the possible aftermath.

The call for the extraordinary meeting was contained in a letter that Cooper and Patricks (and Nolan in the background, for sure) sent to CoDis shareholders on the 19th of May. Months later Paul showed me the letter that Patricks used in the past in Western Australia. Eerily similar, but less polished, it proved to us how premeditated their manoeuvre was.

Dear Shareholders,

We, Roth Cooper and Joel Patricks, in our capacity as shareholders and Directors of CoDis Limited, invite you on the 7th of July to the Boyle Institute Theatre for an extraordinary general meeting.

As you know, CoDis Limited was created on the 2nd of October 1996—on the back of our company SmartInvestments Ltd—by Dr Alba

Gruber and Paul Robertson, respectively CEO and Chairman. Joel and I stayed on as Directors of the Board and as major shareholders.

It went on to resume, from their point of view, the short history of CoDis, including its program.

20 months later, not much has happened. In fact CoDis Ltd is in the red to the tune of $2.4M, a rapidly increasing loss that is burning away our cash at the bank.

We believe that the current administration is lax and ineffectual. The managing director, Dr Alba Gruber, is a former scientist and clearly not used to the pursuit of profit. She is obviously not pushing this enterprise in the right direction.

Mr Paul Creagan, CoDis' chairman, is probably putting much of his energy into other companies: perhaps those that are bigger than CoDis.

We cannot allow this to continue much longer, to witness our assets' erosion to feed the scientific ambition of researchers who have little regard for our funds.

We therefore urge you to vote for the removal of Mr Creagan and Dr Gruber, and for the appointment to the Board of respected businessman Mr. Nolan (see attached CV), according to the following resolutions:

1. *To remove Mr Paul Creagan as Director (Chairman) of the Board of CoDis Limited.*
2. *To remove Dr Alba Gruber as Executive Director of the Board of CoDis Limited.*
3. *To appoint Mr Stanley Nolan as Director of the Board of CoDis Limited."*

Alba and Paul received the letter, distributed on the 19th of May, with consternation. Initially she had one of her peculiar reactions, locking herself into her shell, hands trembling, an automaton walking. Paul expressed his anger and promised to fight on.

After a few days and several meetings, they came up with a plan. Paul took on the task of gathering further support for the stock:

according to PierPont's calculations, Cooper and Patricks' 15% would vote with Nolan's associates 25%, reaching a very critical threshold. Even a few percentage points now could make a difference. It was a case of building up a counter argument, trying to persuade unaligned shareholders to vote for us. Alba had the task of getting letters of support from the four research institutions.

We needed to present a united front, to show that Alba and Paul were respected by those who formed the core of the business, the research leaders.

John Harvey and the CSIRO came up with their written support straight away. They noted that, over their own project, we were very close to signing a lucrative alliance with a large French company, evidence that Dr. Gruber had not been idle. Instead she had been quick to exploit the advantage that the Entomology project was offering.

Leon Kelly was particularly effusive in his praise of CoDis management. He quoted the sensitive involvement of Alba in the recruitment campaign, during which she made herself available to the media to promote the juvenile diabetes' clinical trial.

Carol Latimar's support was unequivocal. She stated that Alba had given her guidance and support, always reminding her group of their duty towards investors. Alba had been particularly careful in calling for results to be achieved with maximum integrity, sensitive in the extreme to the fact that a wrong conclusion could put lives at risk.

But when it came to my turn, Professor Boyle delivered a surprise. He told me without subtleness that our group would not release any declaration of support or otherwise. Alba was astonished and asked to see him. Rob agreed.

"You'd better be coming too," he told me over the phone.

I walked up to the 9th floor, Alba came down from the 10th and we went straight into Rob's office, Denyse posing no barrier for once. Rob started to talk with a calm but cold voice: "You have every right to be surprised, Alba. I understand that."

"And will you have the courtesy to explain why you are doing this, Rob, the only one in four groups to take this stand?" Alba was clearly nervous, her tone including now a metallic background.

"It's very simple, Alba. Remember the rules of least risk? Remember Pascal in the famous quandary on the existence of God? He was, of course, a mathematician, not just a philosopher, so he calculated his risks:

"If he opted for no, and God existed, he would be in trouble; if he opted for yes and God existed, he would be all right; even if God didn't exist, he would still have nothing to worry about. So he said yes, God exists."

Alba was listening so closely she hardly moved.

"In our case," Rob continued, "by doing nothing I run the least risk. If you win, things would go on as before: I'm sure you would honour our agreement anyway. But say you lose, our new masters will appreciate my stand. It's simple."

"I think you are mistaken, Rob, it's not that simple. If they win, they are likely to cut all funding and use the cash otherwise."

"I doubt they'll do that. It would be illegal." Rob seemed sure.

Alba smiled sarcastically, but then opted for the high moral ground: "Don't you understand that they are cynical short-termists who disregard their commitments, that they wouldn't hesitate to destroy our enterprise as they have done with other projects? Don't you know how difficult it is to pursue **White Collar Crime**? Don't you care about what is right or wrong?"

"I can't afford to think about all that. My responsibility is not to my conscience, it is to my institute, to my people and their funding. I have no other ground on which to decide." Rob signaled the end of the discussion.

Alba got up and staggered somewhat. I helped her to the door and to the lift. I had never seen her that way but couldn't find any word that might help.

As we walked towards the lift Alba took my arm, squeezing it with the rhythmic movements of an alternative language. I listened carefully and heard of her great fear. Then she entered the lift and fronted me. Her eyes, still dry for a few more seconds, clearly showed a fear of losing. Losing me as well. Tears then rushed out, cutting with their veil our connection, and the door closed on her before I could utter a word.

Her next outing was in the form of a circular letter, which I received formally, as everybody else. It was a plea she addressed to CoDis' shareholders, sent out together with the three letters of support.

Dear Shareholders,

The letter you have received from two of our Directors is an attempt to convince you to let them seize control of our Board and the Company's assets. Should you vote according to their recommendations, the new Board would have only two independent Directors left, while Messrs Cooper and Patricks would be joined by Mr Nolan to form an absolute majority. The new Board could then take decisions over which you would be largely railroaded.

The argument they used to persuade you to vote for our removal is an irrelevant assumption of profit and loss. Our Prospectus had clearly identified our plan and objectives: to fund research over a three-year period and to develop products with a substantial health benefit for several groups of people.

In no part of the Prospectus did we anticipate to trade or sell our results before the three-year mark. We expected to have to wait for the full period and raised funds accordingly.

In fact, twenty months on, we are on the verge of an important deal, a strategic alliance with a French company that will provide an upfront fee of $5M within a month of signing the agreement.

We have thus exceeded expectations with more than a year to spare. This cannot in any way be construed as ineffective management or unproductive research. To prove this point we also have the support of our joint-venture partners contained in the enclosed letters. They know that funds spent in research cannot be listed as losses; those are expenses that are transformed in know-how and intellectual property assets which have tangible value.

We therefore ask you to defeat the motions that Messrs Cooper and Patricks have submitted to you, so that we can continue without delay our worthy enterprise.

Paul Creagan   *Dr Alba Gruber*
Chairman   *Managing Director*

Under Alba's signature, her title of Managing Director sealed her position from then on in a dramatic way. Her business persona became the only one available to us—even to me: a rigid, forced armor covering her expressions, preventing any direct contact. She seemed to have become captive of a business besieged by those vultures that were attempting to take hold of it.

I would have liked to save her in those days, but as Alba became increasingly isolated and distant, I started to feel angry and powerless. My anger wasn't consciously directed at her, but as she didn't seek comfort from me, it was clear she had decided she wouldn't find any. Perhaps Alba felt powerless herself. Having provided for our projects until now, she must have contemplated the collapse of our plan before our medical teams had been able to extract any meaningful result; statistics are cruel and don't allow conclusions if data are incomplete.

I think of our combined effort in those days: of our precarious research staff with their lab books half-filled yet promising; of our planned experiments carefully calibrated in time with discrete milestones; of our patients' expectations to advance their quests a little at the end of the road. If this enterprise failed, we must have asked, would we be able to set up another one with the same purpose? Nothing was less sure.

***

Thirteen

7 July 1998. The extraordinary general meeting is due to start at 5pm, but I go down there early. The Boyle Institute Theatre is located on the lower ground floor, along with a foyer where tea and biscuits are displayed on side tables and served by two waiters. At the theatre door a man I don't know checks the identity of participants through a list and lets in only shareholders and joint-venture partners.

I enter the theatre, still in dim light, and see Alba with Paul standing at the bottom of the right corridor. They are turning their back to me and I recognise her checkered jacket with colourful specks. Paul has his arm around her shoulders and she looks smaller, somewhat fragile.

There are a few people seated: no one I recognise. On the stage—an elevation of only a foot or so over the rest of the floor—there is a long table where Cooper and Patricks are sitting next to the computer expert/director. He is listening to them but looks aloof, his straight nose sharp as a blade.

Standing about the middle of the table is the physicist/director, her hand clutching a microphone. She is going to chair the meeting because Paul is an interested party. As I pass her and nod, I have this vision of her long curved fingernails grasping the microphone with force, looking like eagle's claws.

Two men, the auditors I met at a management meeting, are seated at one end of the table counting and recounting proxy votes, then checking their hand calculators for totals and comparison, I presume.

I sit down a few rows back and soon more people take their places. Rob comes in and sits next to me without saying a word, but as he approaches, I notice an unusual shade of doubt in his eyes.

Carol, Leon and John come in and sit around us: one behind Rob, one on his left and one on my right. We have surrounded him: that's apt.

Soon more people come in, about seventy on a rough count. Paul and Alba sit in the first row with a couple of suits I don't recognise.

The official part of the meeting is rather short. The Chair reminds those present that each motion will be voted on separately and in the order listed in the letter to shareholders dated 19 May. She explains that present votes will be added to the proxy votes and the results declared by the auditors after appropriate checks. Then she starts reading the motions:

1. "To remove Mr Paul Creagan as Director and therefore Chairman of the Board of CoDis Limited.

"Those in favour raise their hands. Those against? Right. Thank you."

She repeats the same procedure for Resolution 2 and 3. Each of the voting individuals had already registered their votes according to the number of shares they held. So the show of hands is a rather futile exercise, I think. But the auditors continue their count, now flanked by the two suits who, Rob says, are the two parties' lawyers.

In the meantime, Mr Nolan, who is also sitting in the first row, but at the other end of Paul and Alba's, asks to speak. The Chair tells him to approach and take the microphone.

"I would like to say a few words, Madam Chair, to express my sadness at having come to this. I respect Dr Gruber and am convinced that she is nothing other than a good scientist and a passionate supporter of medical research."

He pauses and takes some breath in.

"I am sure that sooner or later we will all need some of the results that she was hoping to achieve and that someone no doubt will some day get. It's just that in these pressed times we cannot afford to fund it the way she wants us to. I'm sorry.

"We have tried to persuade Dr Gruber and Mr Creagan to resign and save this ignominious vote. But she refused and told us that saving face was the least of her worries. I would have liked to come to some arrangement with her, but that was not possible. That's all I have to say."

The Chair grabs the microphone from him and declares that the votes have been counted and confirmed.

"Resolution 1:   3,148 votes for, 2,851 against.
"Resolution 2:   3,107 votes for, 2,892 against.
"Resolution 3:   3,015 votes for, 2,984 against.

"I thus declare all three resolutions passed: Mr Creagan and Dr Gruber are removed as Directors, Mr Nolan is elected as Director."

She is still upstanding when Alba quickly mounts the stage and, walking in front of the table, takes the microphone, then turns towards the audience, holding a piece of paper that CoDis' lawyer gave her:

"Now that it's all over and I'm no longer bound by the reserve of my former positions, I would like to share with you my present thoughts."

The audience murmur but stay still in their seats.

"I don't blame the perpetrators of this coup against Paul and me. They are predators and act according to their primordial instincts. I blame three groups of people for our defeat: the indifferent, the independent and the disloyal.

"The indifferent are those shareholders who did not bother to vote. According to the numbers just revealed, they hold 25% of our stock. Now, considering that the vote against us was about 40%, and the vote for us was around 35%, their abstention was particularly irresponsible.

That they didn't care one way or the other, or couldn't bear to decide, is an indication of their lack of responsibility.

"The independent could be seen in a more positive light; they are the purists who are unaligned, the good directors. Except that they were so close to the workings of this Company, so well informed of the manipulations of these Bandits that they remained independent only because of their allegiance to a pure sense of themselves. In that way they did not pursue the very objective of their role: good governance.

"The disloyal are those who joined us legally in this enterprise but when it came to the test, they decided to pursue their own interests rather than support the objectives they had signed on to.

"Unlike the independent, they failed us for a perceived gain, according to their own calculations of risk in the case of one, of promotion in the case of the other. Both may be mistaken if the new administration changes the operations of this Company.

"Like the independent, though, the disloyal were very close to our business. Their lack of support was therefore extremely damaging because it sowed in the indifferent minds further doubt.

"But enough with blame. I'd like to finish with thanks.

"Thank you, Paul Creagan. You've been a generous, courageous chairman, who in the space of less than two years has turned his accounting mind into a rampart for our enterprise. I'll never forget the support you have lent not only to me, but also to the whole organisation.

"Thank you, project leaders, all four of you, who have continued to work hard at your research, even in the unusual atmosphere of this debacle. You have been my vicarious operators in the world of science, a world where truth is valued above all else. Be sure that despite the current uncertainty and the probable cut in your funds, the research you have accomplished is a stepping-stone for future discoveries.

"A thank you finally to Trevor Sykes, whose PierPont articles—revealing to the public the evidence of underhand activity by covertly associated shareholders—are, I'm sure, the only justice we'll ever get.

"That's all. Thank you for your attention."

Alba downs the microphone and exits through a side door, for good. I get up to follow her but Rob pulls my jacket and I sit down again, feeling angry and powerless.

*

What would have happened if I didn't sit down and followed her instead, trying to comfort her after all? It's clear now, sixteen years later, that I have blamed myself ever since for not doing so. Yet, it would have been the wrong move. Now that the story has unraveled and my memories untangled, the picture of our affair has changed. Now I see more clearly that our perfect agreement was only possible within the borders of our scientific venture. We moved happily only inside that frame. Then, as the venture imploded on that day, our delicate and intimate world could not survive outside.

I reread Alba's letter from Eritrea and return again and again to that first sentence, to the embroidery of our minds and to her way of freezing out in time the magic between us. At last I come to understand her silence, so true to her self, so necessary and honest. I think it was right to sit down and let her escape alone.

***

Epilogue

In fine, why telling this story? What was the reason behind my wanting to write about an event that may appear low stakes if compared to more recent frauds of billions? I don't think it was just my own involvement in it. To show that's the case, I need to try to decouple my own interest in the story from the wider impact it had in those days and later in time. I know of its greater significance and I need to pull that out.

Of course the story had a strong impact on my professional life. If I think of myself at the beginning, I see a purist, a cerebral man who had fun with mental games and visual models, a simple and sure soul. That changed as the story unfolded. No longer concerned with just pure research—with that creative process of theory and proof—I came to appreciate the idea of a scientific enterprise in an applied sense. So much so that, when things went wrong and our venture imploded, going back to academic research was not easy, nor enough.

I left the Boyle Institute soon after and took my Fellowship elsewhere, completing in time a moderately successful research program. But my heart was no longer in that game and I turned to science writing and journalism. After all, good science and good journalism have something in common: they both pursue the truth to its nearest approximation. And that is what I like to do.

But the more negative impact of CoDis' demise lies elsewhere. The debacle, with its facts and rumours, became for a while an incessant talking point inside the research community. It was really unprecedented: large funds in the bank, legally pledged to research in four different establishments, disappearing all of a sudden in the middle of the program, leaving costs uncovered and scientists out of their jobs. In the mind of young researchers the blame was generalised, with the finger pointed to private funding of research, while fear of the business element broke out and finance took the appearance of a magnet for dirty tricks. Who would want to work for a Biotech venture soon after that?

Even worse for the Australian Biotech industry, investors became wary and more reticent to fund it, unsure as they were of the reasons behind CoDis' demise. Shy of the courts, they saw no point in spending time and money trying to find out what really happened to CoDis after the Bourse Brigands took over. They would have learnt that the new masters—with Lyanne promoted to chief executive for the transition—quickly changed the nature of the business from Biotech to a wine packaging and distribution company. Many millions changed pockets in just one transaction, as the Bandits sold their own fledgling wine business to what was formerly known as CoDis.

But the investment community had no time for these details. They filed the change as a loss for Biotech and a remarkable one at that: as they recognised competence and expertise in CoDis, they concluded that there was something wrong with Biotech in general. And they swayed away from it for a while.

So, when I think of the three sly men who met at a suburban club and planned to target our carefully assembled research venture, I agree that it was a small event. Except that it caused disproportionate collateral damage.

****

Cellular Gardens Where the Breathing Begins

Memory of Nature View

Memory of Nature (detail 1)

Memory of Nature (detail 2)

Eve's Speed

ONE

9 June 2017. What a change in the periphery! Crossing it by train today, I remember how it used to look when I was living in Paris twenty-five years ago. Then, boulevards on the outskirts of the city cut through ugly suburbs, occasionally splitting into slower arteries around them. On the main route, millions of cars crisscrossed the fast lanes, creating traffic that shook the nerves of the drivers and sounded furious.

People living in outer, leafier suburbs had to pass by cheap apartment blocks cramming the periphery to the east of Paris. Converging on the city, towards government offices or companies' headquarters, masses of middle class citizens poured gases and particles directly on to those sad homes where small balconies, if they existed, could not be opened to the thick air.

Living in the centre of Paris, a sensitive stranger could not avoid being touched by the contrast. In fact, the beauty of central Paris acted like a border: those who left it behind to enter the periphery were inevitably gripped by a sense of dread; in the opposite direction, those who reached it felt instantly the force of privileged territory. The beauty of Paris was really a trap. By leaving it and aiming for the countryside and fresh air, one had to pay the price of losing sight of the finest architecture. The prize was green nature, but human genius was left behind.

In the years since, things have changed. The periphery boulevards are unclogged, running in parallel with small, clean and cheerfully colored monorail trains driven on magnetic levitation. Few cars are in sight, as the center of Paris is closed to ordinary traffic, and those huge car lots have been turned into amenities and green parks where people wander during lunchtime.

The apartment blocks in the periphery, newly rebuilt, have nice terraces lined with pot plants and the odd tennis court underneath. Bicycle lanes are everywhere and cyclists wear rubber headgear that makes them look like baseball players. A sense of human, direct action pervades the place and helps to create a pleasant atmosphere.

Of course this may be the static view of a tourist whose superficial impressions cannot be well informed. Now there are other worries on my mind as I sit in the train crossing the periphery of Paris. I'm heading for Creteil to listen to the verdict of a dear friend who will stand today in the local court for the final session of her trial. The trial is in its second year, so it's not the first time I've come to visit Eve. As her scientific mentor, I have been considered one of the main witnesses to her act. Not that I was physically present when it happened: she was very much on her own. I was very close to her in the preceding months, and one of the few people she confided in. Despite, or perhaps because of, our age difference Eve trusted me. The mentoring developed slowly over the years while we gradually realized that our scientific views and ideals were quite similar.

In my case, I sensed no comparable closeness to my own children, who had grown intellectually distant and had interests far removed from science. As for Eve, she found her parents, friends of mine and scientists themselves, too pragmatic for her principles and devoid of the ideals she believed in. So my mentoring her and our friendship fulfilled mutual needs that some people misunderstood in the usual trite way: the only explanation they could find for the relationship between this older man and young, attractive Eve. We didn't care about the rumors and would not relent. Her parents understood, in fact they were glad that I was lending an ear to Eve's thinking. For her part, my wife was simply relieved at being spared my interminable outpouring of views and reflections.

For a long time Eve and I discussed and modified our views on several subjects, but at one point we came to focus on a limited area and one particular question: to what extent do scientists have the right to help modify human nature? We were used to the view of medical doctors; there were many of them trying their hands at part-time research in our laboratories. For them, it was all clear-cut. They had taken up the Hippocratic oath of working to save lives and to spare pain: that was it. But we human scientists fronted more unmapped territory.

My discipline, neurology, and Eve's embryology were particular beneficiaries of rapid technological advances for which no one was ready: not the ethics committees of our research establishments and certainly not the law. So we had no guidance, while new technologies gave us the tools to increase our understanding of human biology and provided us with the means to intervene and change it. When something went wrong, as in the case of disease or congenital defects, there was no question that we would work to find remedies. But when scientists found that a biological improvement on normality was suddenly possible and desirable, what should they do with it? We were the guardians of that Aladdin's lamp: should we stroke it or not?

We found ourselves slightly marginalized from the main scientific stream. Most scientists, Eve's parents included, would not discuss these issues in a hypothetical way. They did not like to anticipate; they followed evidence step by step in an appropriate quest to understand and apply new knowledge to current needs.

On the other hand, Eve and I liked to build conjectures on hypothetical issues, as we were very conscious of the possibility that future biology would create different, more complex needs and greater opportunities. The scope of our private discussions grew for a long time in an abstract form. Then one day Eve stumbled on a real example.

***

TWO

On March 1, 2013 a biological 'incident' showed up under the careful watch of embryologist Eve Latimar. She checked and checked, there was no doubt, it was an extraordinary finding: two embryos with a mutation that has never been seen before.

That's how I started my popular press article on Eve's discovery. I had turned my hand to journalism, following belatedly in my father's footsteps, and was enjoying my new career as a science writer.

The story begins one morning as I am sitting at my desk in Sydney, pondering about my next article. Eve calls me and tells me the general fact, no details. I am an old friend and colleague of her mother. I've seen Eve grow up from a tiny bundle in a portable cot—sometimes visiting our lab—to a determined and committed scientist. She now works at the Sydney headquarters of a large medical company specializing in IVF research and service to the community of infertile couples.

"Would you report this news when we're ready?" she asks. "I'll tell Leo your role is not negotiable." Leo is her boss and clearly she wants to keep control on this thing: she'll have it with me, she knows. I agree straight away.

"Sorry, but I can't tell you the details now," Eve says, "just in case. Listen, I'll send you a few websites so that you can brush up on your embryology. Then you'll be ready when we call you."

I warn my editor in person: there may be an exclusive story ahead in the next few days.

"I hope you'll make room for this," I say. He is curious: wants to know more, but I really can't tell. He's always been somewhat suspicious of scientific journalism, mine in particular, with all those qualifications, where nothing is clear-cut despite all the evidence-based arguments. But I guess he knows that certain biomedical stories—like those on stem cells and therapeutic cloning—have attracted a lot of interest lately, perhaps more for their ethical import than anything else. He agrees.

Checking my email, I notice a message from Eve. She's sent it from her private address, not the Company's, to my encrypted account. She's being careful: good on her. The websites she recommends are from MedReviews' and Nature Highlights' sections. I print out some forty pages as I can't read all this on screen since my eyes have become sensitive to that light after so many years of exposure. With an advanced experimental process we are trying, the paper can be recycled at will, removing ink in a dry bath and reusing the sheets forever. The ink is biodegradable and once removed it can be fed to plants.

I spend the evening on the embryology papers. There is so much I didn't know! The field has grown incredibly since I was involved in research ten years ago. Clearly, the genetics of embryos is most advanced—I expected that—but the epigenetics! That's where they've made the biggest advances, showing how much genes are under external chemical control. A far more uncertain world is opening before my eyes. I had always been pretty sure of my biology and in particular of genetics. Now genes seem far more fragile than I thought, more vulnerable in their switching at the whim of certain chemical conditions.

It takes me a while to absorb the molecular biology data of the papers arguing for new mechanisms that must be involved in the control of genes by epigenetic conditions: what a maze! Fortunately I follow the gist, although some technical details are now beyond me. Not to worry. I am used to summing up, reaching a conclusion and taking home essential messages.

One conclusion from those papers on the website is that, while embryos develop, some of their genes may be turning on or off depending on the conditions that surround them in the womb. Therefore the life habits of their bearers—the parents—are really critical for the formation of the embryo. Certain habits may help to turn on or off certain genes in the embryo, or even before that, in sperm and eggs.

I ring Eve at home early next morning. "Eve, I'm ready when you are. Any progress with Leo?"

"He's in shock and wants to think it over for a day or two. Yes, I know, we're wasting time, but he wants to discuss it with the Company's Ethics Committee before going public."

Leo shocked? It must be a really extraordinary event to move such a man. I've heard Eve describing her boss as a brilliant, powerfully egocentric, control maniac and greedy as well. Years ago, Eve commented on the formation of the Ethics Committee: representatives of the three monotheistic religions plus lawyers and leaders from ethical organizations, they make up an influential, respected group who use a sophisticated procedure to deal with delicate issues that are presented to the Company.

I think it's a good idea to consult them: they would work out the arguments, the answers to objections from various contrarians. If of course the Committee concluded in positive terms, which wasn't always the case. That might take more than a couple of days. I warn my editor.

Eve calls me the next day from her mobile. The line is not good. Noise creeps behind her weak voice.

"Where are you?" I ask.

"In the coffee shop on the Company's square. You know, I'm close to panicking. This thing might slip from my hands. After all it's work I do for the Company; we've got an agreement. We **have** to share invention data, royalties and so on, but this isn't really an invention. Of course I found it, I've grown it and observed it. It's my discovery all right, but they might take it off my hands . . . . and I'm scared of that."

She sounds confused. I have to help her, as I've done many times before.

"Eve, come to Martin Place—it's only a few minutes away—and we'll talk. Hang on: are the embryos coded? You haven't disclosed the codes to anyone, have you?"

"NO, no," she says "I've put the vitrified embryos in two canisters, and the canisters back in a liquid nitrogen container with heaps of others. No one knows which embryos are which and I always carry the ipad with the codes. OK, see you in five."

She's just revealed that she broke the Company's lab procedure. Codes of identification should be entered in the master file, an intranet repository of data. Eve has not entered her codes. She may be found out soon. We need to talk about that.

A slight figure disguising a strong will, Eve turns the corner and soon faces me. We greet affectionately and I sense her tension. Her eyes have changed from a golden color to a flat green; her dark-brown hair looks opaque, lifeless. We sit down on a bench facing the old post office, now a Macquarie Energy building.

"Eve, we need to work out a strategy to gain time."

She agrees.

"Have you got any proof to back your claim?" I ask.

"Oh, yes, it's all documented in time-lapsed photography," she explains. "I've got two embryos with the same pattern of growth. Both were checked with photos every hour."

"For how long?"

"Just twenty four hours, but a lot happens to embryos in that short time."

"Is this routine?"

"No, no; it's just that the day before I was growing the twins of the same two embryos when a strange thing about their growth hit me. It was completely unexpected."

"And you weren't ready with the camera set-up."

"That's right, and I couldn't do it then, so I decided to thaw the other two, set them up for lapsed photography and follow their growth very carefully. They behaved exactly in the same way! But I can't tell more now."

"It's OK, Eve, I can wait, but you need to take some precaution. Why don't you take your documents to a patent attorney? I can organize an appointment with someone I trust, if you want me to."

Eve agrees but is still tense, I can tell from the way she clutches the handles of her bag. I put my hand over her raised knuckles and squeeze.

"Remember '*Bacteria*'? I say.

She smiles. It's one of our earliest memories together. She must have been six or seven. I was visiting her home, her mother busy getting lunch ready, Eve playing about in the kitchen. After a while, as we chatted, Eve picked up a piece of biscuit from the floor and was about to put it in her mouth when her mother stopped her:

"Bacteria!" she said in a loud voice, "they'll make you sick!" Eve froze, the gingerbread fragment flat on her open hand, moist eyes looking at me.

"Come with me in the garden," I said "we'll bury the biscuit in the ground. Bacteria, you know, can be good for plants."

That calmed her down, as we dug together the soil with a little spade she normally used at the beach.

"Yes, I remember." Eve says.

"Now, let's solve this together as we did then." I feel her knuckles relaxing.

"I'm glad I called you." She seems to be talking to herself.

"Eve, how are you going to avoid entering your data in the system?"

"Oh, it's OK." She has regained confidence. "We're allowed to embargo data that we're unsure of, or want anyway to check further. And we're not required to enter illustrations like photos; it's optional. I guess this got the tick as a saving measure but it suits me fine right now."

We decide to meet again for lunch the following day, same place.

"Let's avoid leaving traces of this on phones or e-mails," I suggest.

"Fine," she says, "I'll bring some *budini di riso*. I'll bake them tonight."

"And I'll brew some of my Ethiopian coffee and will bring it in a thermos," I add. We smile and breathe in as if smelling already the familiar combination while we walk away.

I am busy, though, and we meet only three days later. Eve has gone alone with her material to see the patent attorney. She is satisfied at least about the safety of her evidence, locked away in a cabinet now, although the embryos are still at the Company's premises. Being unidentifiable, they should be safe too.

Over lunch on the same bench we enjoy our shared food and drinks like never before. She fills me in on the attorney's comments. What she's done is legitimate.

Protecting her own work while not making any exclusive claims to the findings—too early for that—is within her rights. She is reassured. He's also explained that patent protection is not appropriate at this stage. This is because she doesn't know how the 'incident' occurred. Patenting is possible only if you have sufficient detail to allow anyone skilled in that technology to reproduce it.

No, it's not a question of patenting, he told her, and that was even better. Otherwise she would have to assign part of the rights to the Company according to her job contract.

No, in this case it would be just her discovery, for which she would get scientific recognition if and when she could trace back cause and mechanism.

Eve seems very excited at the prospect of further work which might require collaborative efforts. She starts talking of her colleagues overseas with whom she liked working.

"Eve, what about the Ethics Committee?" I ask.

'Oh yes, I meant to tell you. Sorry. Well, they are very divided and haven't been able to reach a consensus. Some members want us to terminate the experiment immediately; others see some value in trying to find out how such an incredible event could have happened."

"And Leo, what does he want to do?"

"Oh," she smiles, "he's declared his hand: he thinks it's a great opportunity for the patients, that is, for our market. He said: 'If we could find out what happened and were able to reproduce it with other embryos, that would give us a strong competitive advantage!'"

"But do you think you can?"

"I don't know. I've got no idea. But maybe we could test the embryos' genes first to see what changed to make them so extraordinary. That would take months but is feasible. In the meantime we could go back to study the parents' lifestyle."

'Why?" I am intrigued.

"See, fortunately we have two different embryos with different parents. Statistically it's not much, but better than just one. I mean it's happened twice, so it's not just a freak accident. As the two embryos have the same growth pattern, we could find out the cause by their similarity, and in turn, by their difference from all other 'normal' embryos."

"What about disclosure?" I press on: "Has the Ethics Committee made any recommendation about going public?"

"They are divided four to four. In fact, Leo is also a Committee member and he's got the ninth vote. He's obliquely referred to that and I guess he'd want the publicity. But at the time we spoke, he said he hadn't made up his mind. He's cautious, so he'll want to wait for the go-ahead from the Company's board of directors."

"Anyway," I say keenly, "I'd better get ready. Listen, I thought of publishing a straight interview with Leo, if he agrees. Normally, I'd report various opinions from experts, cross check and so on. But we don't have the time. We'd better go out with the news straight from one source—your lab."

"Fine by me." Eve smiles broadly.

"If you are allowed to sit through the interview, just to fill in some details, we can give Leo the bigger space for now. He should be enticed by that. Do you want to ask him?"

"I'll try," says Eve. "In the meantime, think about this; the parents of the two embryos are quite unusual."

"What do you mean?"

"Each member of the two couples is in the same business. That is, man and wife are in the same line of work: one couple in the currency derivatives market and the other in elite athletics. Some of their lifestyle habits may explain it all!"

Back in the office, I am busy with other work but Eve's story will have priority. I'd drop everything for this, and two days later I have to. Eve rings me at night.

"More developments," she says. "Internal sequel. Can we meet tomorrow, first thing?"

"Of course, Eve, but let's change places. Join me in the foyer of the Chinalco building on the other side of Martin Place. I know the security guard there; he'll let us use their comfortable couches."

She agrees.

I arrive there first and exchange pleasantries with the guard. He nods and I take a seat in the far left corner of the foyer. It has a cathedral-high ceiling contrasted by a steel structure rising from the centre of the atrium in the shape of a tree trunk with branches expanding towards the southern and eastern corners of the ceiling. There won't be an echo here.

I see Eve entering from the revolving door. She hesitates and looks up at the strange structure. I walk towards her.

"It looks, on a much larger scale, like the artery aorta," she says, "and the branches are similar to the coronary arteries that surround the heart of the mature fetus hanging upside down in the uterus."

Some perspective, I think.

She starts talking as we walk towards the couch.

"I was invited to a bit of the Board of Directors meeting!" she exclaims. "They wanted to ask me some questions. You know, it was very intimidating. To start with, I'd never seen that meeting room. It's enormous! A table with forty chairs, abstract paintings on the walls, just one window stretching a full wall looking over the square from the 36th floor. And the Chairman, scary!"

"Who's he?" I ask. "A doctor?"

"No, no," she says excitedly, "he's a financier from the very top end of town; at the beginning, he was just an accountant—I've read this in the annual report—who made the right investment during the energy upheaval of the '00s. He backed an obscure company that had come up with a novel fusion technology that is promising, but still experimental."

"Yes," I say, "the new atomic energy source."

"Well," Eve continues, "apparently he and Leo were students together, I mean in the same College, playing rugby for Sydney University, and that's how they got to become good friends. Tim told me all this."

Tim is a colleague I've met at Eve's place. He works in the same Company and is one level higher than Eve. I suspect some association between the two, more than a working relationship, but don't mention it.

"Well," Eve continues, "the Chairman started asking me questions: 'Miss Latimar,' he said after a few nice words of greeting, 'could you tell us if you've divulged your information to any outsider?'

"I replied no to him, and that's true, don't you think? I haven't told you the actual facts, just the general circumstances, haven't I?"

"Of course, Eve, you've done the right thing," I reassure her.

"Then the Chairman went on to ask me what I expected from this set of events. I told him that I wanted recognition of my primary role, undiluted."

"Did Leo agree to that?"

"I don't know; he didn't say anything. Then I said that I'd want to be funded adequately to study the causes and mechanisms of this phenomenon. The Chairman didn't flinch and asked if I had an idea of the sum involved, but I didn't, so he suggested that I worked on a plan and a budget.

"Then another Director, who chairs the Audit and Risk Committee of the Company, started querying me. He wanted to cover all kinds of risk we could be running."

"Are there any?"

"Oh, plenty, according to him. Say if the embryos died, if they were implanted and caused health problems for the mother, if there could be payments sought by her on account of the favorable publicity to the Company if successful, and all sorts of other risks."

"And do you know if any of those apply?"

"No, of course not, but Leo helped me by saying that the questions would be passed on to the Risk Management Task Force."

"Ooph!"

"Yeah. I don't need that sort of responsibility, for sure."

"And then?"

"Well, the Chairman wrapped it up by saying that I should be very careful in my moves, something like: always consult with the Managing Director (i.e. Prof. Leo Vladov), meet the Ethics Committee's chair and try to understand more broadly what's at stake."

"So were you happy with that?"

"Sort of, but I still don't know if Leo told the Board what's the matter with my embryos."

"In any case," I assure her, "the directors can't talk; they made a pledge to the Company and can't divulge what they've learnt from the MD, even if he's gone into details, which I doubt."

Eve is sitting next to me with a remote look on her face now. She seems worried and unhappy.

"How are you coping with all this attention?" I ask her.

"Oh, it's OK, but it's weird: totally out of my normal ways. And I'm terribly worried I'll lose the plot. You know, the meetings, the questions, the interventions; all that makes me feel this matter is everyone's. That seems to curb my input, my freedom to act, to decide the next move. And I don't know how to fight that." She looks dejected.

"Don't go there, Eve; there's no need to feel helpless. There's a lot on your side. First, they wouldn't be so careless as to move you from your position. You've been handling these embryos, you know what to do with them."

"That's for sure."

"But that's not all; you've got international collaborations going, and that should help to resolve the questions and find the cause for what happened."

"All true." Eve nods feebly.

"And then," I seem unable to stop, "of course there are legal avenues. These days, scientists are in a strong position, legally I mean. Think of the Biotechnology Property Rights Act, which should be passed this year. That gives researchers, no matter where they work, rights that are similar to copyrights in art and literature. Remember how I was involved in the campaign leading to the preparation of the Bill? Your work diaries and your photos are your copyright and they are in safe hands."

She nods more convincingly and looks relieved.

"Have you talked to Tim about this?" I ask.

"No, not at all," she says in a worried tone: "He'll be very cross when he finds out. You know, we're very close but I've realized he's not very important to me. If I had to choose between him and my work, I'd let him go."

"It must be difficult not to talk about an event like this with your peers. Are you sure you can't trust Tim with this?"

"No, no." Eve is adamant. "There could be professional jealousy, very likely. Tim is the director of the Stem Cell Division and this thing, even though it belongs to the Embryology Department, could have a use for stem cell developments. Our group could become the primary movers in *his* field! He wouldn't take that nicely."

"So," I conclude, "you are heading towards a break-up."

"Probably," she concurs. "You know, this incident has exposed the depth, really the shallow depth of my feelings for him. My next man will be from an entirely different milieu." She smiles suddenly. "Have you got any juicy, available colleague at the paper?"

"I'll look out for him, Eve."

She keeps her smile. For the first time in weeks, her eyes glitter and regain a transparent light.

"Life is certainly going to change for me," she says.

***

Three

May 3, 2013. An unknown woman is at the other end of my phone.

"Good morning," she says in a neutral, professional voice, "my name is Penelope and I'm ringing to arrange an appointment on behalf of Professor Vladov. It seems you're going to interview him."

"That's right."

"Well, would tomorrow morning at 10 suit you?" she inquires.

"Yes, fine by me, but before you go, Penelope, let me tell you how I plan to proceed: first, there will be photo taking. I'll be there with a photographer and a sound technician for the recording, since our radio associates may decide to broadcast the interview. I'd also like Eve Latimar to be present to answer some questions and of course to sit for the photos. Is that OK?"

"Yes," she says with a touch of impatience in her voice, "Professor Vladov anticipated all that."

We agree to meet at the reception desk on the 36th floor. I am excited. Finally the day has come to unravel this mystery. I go and see my editor.

"We're on, tomorrow."

"What time?"

"AM."

"Great," he says, "in time for the evening run. We'll print an extract of the interview for the evening issue and the full interview in the next morning edition. And online, of course."

He is satisfied. The printed medium is enjoying a new spring of life after the confirmation, in longitudinal studies, of screen damage to the eyes and spinal cord. What's more, media reforms have strengthened our proprietor's hand and the new broadsheet, *Australia Now,* dominates the print media nationally, with inserts on State affairs.

The evening edition, an elegant tabloid, has news extracts and photos on the front page, but it is mainly made up of opinion pieces (crocodiles), which have been prepared beforehand by experts who have agreed to be published only in connection with the news they relate to by theme. It was my editor's idea (a modification of *The Wall Street Journal*) and it works well.

"Which crocodile do you want to use?" the editor asks me.

"I've picked up three," I say, "and I'll decide with Eve which one is the most relevant to the interview theme. And of course," I add slowly but firmly, "I don't want any sub-editing; this is delicate material. You only need to give me space and I'll close myself both copies, including the titles."

"OK," he says, "it's your game."

Eve rings in the evening. "Are you ready?" she asks.

"As much as I can be, but tell me, Eve, which of these three articles would fit your story for the evening edition?"

"What do they talk about?"

"One is on the rights of women vis-à vis implantation: who can decide, who can oppose it, what to do with surplus embryos, etcetera. The second is on the technical side: the statistics of IVF, the success rates, the side effects, and all the improvements of the past five years. The third is about the ethical aspect: the Catholic Church's view versus the other Churches', but also the lay ethical angle on the rights of an embryo."

"Right, good. Any of them could do," she says. "But maybe the third one is the least relevant now. And the second is too dry for an evening paper. I'd say the first one, if it's well balanced."

"Yes, it is," I confirm, "and quite subtle too. Another thing before you go, Eve: make sure you do your hair. It's normally the first thing people notice in newspaper photos. And very little make-up, as usual; I want you to be you."

We exchange goodnights; we both need a good sleep.

But I re-read the first opinion piece. I cut some paragraphs out, where the rights of single people to have IVF are discussed. This is certainly not relevant to our news. I send the new version in an email attachment to the author, asking for her permission, explaining the general reasons and announcing the publication the following day. In the morning, before I leave, her answer is there with an enthusiastic approval. Great. I bounce it on to my editor.

I've prepared a series of questions for this interview, but am sure I'll have to improvise once I'm told the exact nature of the phenomenon. While most of the questions will be put to Vladov, I try to structure the sequence so that the actual disclosure comes from Eve.

The crew's electric van picks me up from home and the three of us arrive ahead of time at the Company's building in the City. They chose that location because it was convenient for the Macquarie Street gynecologists to shuttle from their private surgeries, and also because most of their IVF clients worked in the CBD. It's an elegant but not glitzy establishment.

Penelope meets us in the reception room. She looks even sterner than she sounded on the phone.

"The interview will take place in the external laboratory of the Embryology Division," she says. "There won't be access to the internal laboratory, as that is high containment area, but you'll be shown all you need anyway."

Penelope escorts us to a lower level, where we meet Eve.

"You know Dr Latimar, I believe," she says and disappears discreetly.

Eve takes us through a long corridor to a corner room where there is a Laminar flow cabinet, a scanning microscope and a small incubator.

The photo shoot is set up and, with all the equipment, the four of us already fill the room when Leo appears at the door. I've seen his photo before.

"Good morning, Professor Vladov," I say, smiling slightly. Eve has warned me that he dislikes flattery or excessive amiability. He is from a White Russian family who migrated to Australia when he was five, after roaming Eastern Europe from the time the Bolsheviks took over.

He is taller than me, and as we shake hands I notice, at my level, his impeccable taste in ties: this one an exquisite, brilliant blue background with little brown umbrellas, all open.

"Professor Vladov," I say, "do you mind if we take first the photos of the scientist at her bench, and to save time, start her part of the interview?"

"Go ahead," he tells me in a reluctant tone.

"Eve," I say, "we'd like shots of you pretending to culture an embryo under the Laminair hood, then looking into the microscope, and finally fronting the camera. In the meantime, I'll ask you a couple of questions, OK?"

Eve nods and sits at the hood after taking a small dish from the incubator. The dish contains a strange vessel that is transparent and sits in liquid medium. I signal the sound technician to start recording.

"Dr Latimar, you are an embryologist and have worked in this company for the past seven years, growing embryos for IVF. Can you tell us more?"

"Yes, we've made a lot of progress in this area over that period: we've developed new culture media, a special minicrib where the embryos grow, a method of vitrification that preserves the embryos in storage, and so on."

"And now, what have you uncovered after all these improvements?"

"Well, until now, with these techniques we were able to handle embryos better, so we've had a much higher number of live births than other clinics. But something out of the ordinary happened a few weeks ago. After extracting stem cells from two embryos, as I often do, I found that these stem cells multiplied very rapidly, much more than usual.

"Then I looked at the two embryos themselves and noticed that they showed an amazing fast growth, phenomenal in fact. To put it in perspective, at this rate of growth their pregnancy term would be reduced from nine to five-six months!"

Here it is, the news. I didn't expect it to be so simple and yet so important. I hesitate and look at Vladov. His face has red blotches now, spread around his cheeks; I notice them as he faces me. He turns his head slightly to look over his shoulder and rapidly brushes off with his hand the fleck sitting on his dark blue suit.

I signal to my crew the change of subject. They start shooting photos of him as he peers over Eve's head at the microscope. The recorder is on.

"Professor Vladov, what is your view of this finding? Do you share Dr Latimar's enthusiasm and excitement?"

"Clearly, it's something unprecedented. It hasn't been described anywhere else in the world; we checked extensively. We've been striving in the past to foster the wellbeing of embryos and we've devised many improvements in their conditions over the past twenty-five years. And, let me tell you, much before young Eve appeared on the scene, we made real inroads.

"But of course," his voice turns its tone to a higher pitch, "Eve was the lucky one who happened to be in charge of these two particular embryos."

"Is this something you have been trying to obtain: a speedier pregnancy for the convenience of your patients/mothers to be? An experiment in epigenetics?"

"Of course not. We've never contemplated such a thing. And we've never been asked to. Normally a six-month pregnancy is viewed as a problem of premature birth and no one dreamed of wishing it. But this, if all goes well, would be a normal term, a fully developed baby after five to six months. Can you imagine the benefit for the mother, most probably a professional woman, saving a third of her time on the pregnancy, shaving off a third of all the side effects that even the most uneventful term entails?"

"Have you advised the two couples involved, Professor Vladov?"

"We have. We couldn't let them learn this from the media, could we? And it's necessary to disclose the identity of the embryos: otherwise all other patients could have imagined being the parents of the phenomenon. But we did this under obligation of secrecy."

"What was the couples' reaction? Can you tell us if they intend to go ahead with their IVF plans?"

"I can't disclose it. It's up to them to make statements to the media. But they were certainly excited at the news, and it's possible that, in the event, they might be inclined to change their plans and perhaps modify the timing of the embryo implantation in the uterus.

"I can't say in these two cases, but sometimes women defer and have their embryos stored for a later date. Now the curiosity might make them change their mind."

"By the way, Professor, can you tell me if it's true that you are considering serial twin implantations?"

"Well, I wouldn't say considering it. We know it's possible to form twins in vitro, namely to split an embryo at around the 4 cell stage, normally on day 2 post conception, and form twins. Then each twin can be grown up to day 5, normally a ball containing about 100 cells, and one embryo is implanted while the other is stored for another time.

"Although we haven't done this yet, it is conceivable that we could implant the identical twins at a distance of, say, 2 years from each other and have two identical babies 2 years apart."

"Why would you want to do that?"

"For convenience, mainly. The patient would not have to go through the stimulation cycle again, although of course we collect and store several different embryos from the same woman in one stimulation cycle for future implantations. But imagine the case of a family with a genetic, inheritable disease and only one of the available embryos happens to be viable and normal. In this case, twinning could solve the problem of a subsequent normal pregnancy."

"In your fast-growing embryos, do you envisage the possibility of twinning?"

"As a matter of fact, Eve has already done it. She split the original two embryos in four as soon as she realized an unusual growth. You see, she didn't know what would happen. Then she grew two and stored the other two, very quickly, as soon as she realized the accelerated growth. You need to understand that you can't let embryos grow in vitro beyond a certain size, say 100 cells. The growth has to be stopped by vitrification unless one were ready to be implanted, which wasn't the case, of course. Not yet."

"What do you expect will happen to those embryos once implanted? Would they continue at an accelerated growth rate?"

"Of course we don't know until we've done it. But there is no logical reason why they should change their growth pattern. You see, there is clearly an epigenetic effect here. I mean, the growth, the cell cycle is governed by a number of genes. For some reason, these genes were altered by the action of external chemicals and their speed up-regulated. The reason must reside in their parents, not in our culture conditions, since thousands of other embryos in our hands had a normal growth. So, implanting the embryos where they originally came from shouldn't change their growth pattern."

"Professor, do you think there will be ethical objections to the potential implantations?"

"I am sure there will be. And everyone will consider very carefully the possible consequences, not only from an ethical point of view, but also from a medical risk perspective, for both mother and child."

"Lastly, which application of this phenomenon do you expect to be most time effective: the stem cell production or the shorter pregnancy term?"

"Probably the stem cell production. You see, we've already got that going and provided we can maintain some cells at the stem level, that is pluri-potent, not committed to a particular cell type, we can keep growing and expanding them at will. With Eve's 'incident', we might have found a serendipitous way to produce large numbers of stem cells, the holy grail of regenerative medicine. We could then start to use them for diabetes patients, for instance, or patients with heart infarction, or even neurological degeneration."

"While the pregnancies?"

"The pregnancies, on the other hand, are still hypothetical. We don't know if we'll be allowed to implant the embryos, given their extraordinary growth. We don't know if the mother's physiology can sustain the rapid growth or if the embryos will result in live births. There is a lot of work ahead on this front. But first we should try to understand what has changed, the cause of the accelerated growth, the mechanism involved."

"An ongoing story, then. We look forward to hearing more of it in the future. Thank you, Professor Vladov."

He nods, rises from his chair and walks towards Eve. Penelope suddenly reappears and escorts us to the lift, silently.

*

On the way back to the paper there is a sense of elation in the van, the sound technician and the photographer taking turns in chanting:

"We did it!"

The phrase rises and falls in my mind many times as if wanting to check that it has really happened at last. Yes! We have the scoop.

And then, a new nagging thought surfaces, uncalled. Professor Vladov's remark, 'Young Eve was the lucky one', was meant clearly to put Eve's role in perspective: just a stroke of luck. But there she is now with a big discovery in her hands and the celebrity that will inevitably ensue. Did our professor doubt that she could handle the enormity of it all? I do. She has had a very protected life so far: no notable setbacks, no difficulty she could learn from, no major mistakes. And this would not be the right time to start making them.

Inevitably my mind goes back to some of my memories of Eve as a young girl. I remember Mark, her father, worried one day about her:

"Eve is maturing fast," he said, while watching her fondly as she left our dining room to join my son, Max. "At times I think she doesn't have enough fun for her age."

Maturing. Mark chose the word well and gave me the sense that Eve was getting there intellectually, already capable of holding her point in a conversation with us. From the height of a distant time though, I see her intellectual maturity far from being matched by an emotional one.

On that day Mark should not have worried. After all, Eve went to play with Max and our dog in the park, having a little girl's fun. But perhaps he kept protecting her too much, loving his only child so perfectly that in the outside world she cruised through superficial attachments without really growing up.

Perhaps that was also Eve's way to save more space for her intellectual pursuits, in part turning to me for my mental games, my views on the brain and the mind, my speculations about a certain biological future.

My error was to take her on board, putting a risky distance between her intellectual sail and her emotional self, which remained undeveloped onshore.

***

Four

After a brief stopover in my editor's bunker to fill him in on the interview, I am back at my desk. This is my great new toy, a source of unashamed pride and fun. I am the only one at the paper to have been given this experimental machine on account of my neurological training. It is one of the earliest prototypes of voice recognition systems for the print media and I've had it for about six months now. Most of the teething problems with the software have been resolved with additional bits of artificial intelligence, a few more neural networks, and the computer has learnt to understand my voice perfectly and act on my command.

The desk itself is like an architect's drawing board, with variable inclinations. The board is made of a glassy block that lights up to a blue screen with windows of different sizes. A dual hard disk is incorporated underneath for more memory and other features. There are no keypads, just touch circles, mostly control modes rather than letters. I select the speech recognition mode and start talking.

"Hi, Ordi, I am back and will work with you for a while. We have to get the evening story ready in an hour."

[Ordi is, of course, a contraction of the word *ordinateur,* French for computer. I've always preferred that description: ordering, putting files in order. I feel it closer to my use of the machine than to compute, count, calculate. Pronounced in the French way, it also sounds like *'or, dit',* meaning 'now, tell (me)', a frequent call during my searches.]

=OK=

Ordi doesn't speak and his words on the screen are rigorous and economical. Just enough to show its understanding.

"I'll tell you the plan. I intend to dictate first a short introduction to the article and then I'll download directly the sound recording of the interview I've done this morning. You'll incorporate title, intro, and do the layout, typesetting, the whole lot for the morning and part for the evening edition. Then you'll show it to me as a draft."

=READY=

"Another thing, Ordi. In the interview you'll hear two other voices alternating with mine, so I'll put you on intermitting mode."

=RIGHT=

This mode allows multiple repetitions of the 'foreign' fragments, while mine is run just once now that Ordi can perfectly recognize my voice. I put on my special helmet to concentrate. Made of dark, molded, thin Perspex, with inbuilt microphone and headphones, it allows me visual and sound insulation from the busy, open-space office filled with rows of desks and people chatting or typing along.

"Go, Ordi. Title: **Young Scientist Finds Human Mutation**.

"Intro: *On March 1, 2013 at her lab, under her microscope, in two Petri dishes, embryologist Eve Latimar uncovered a biological 'incident'. She checked and confirmed. Without doubt it was an extraordinary finding: two embryos, out of the thousands she had grown over the years, showed a pattern that had never been seen before.*

"She told me just this much before our interview this morning in the premises of the Sydney company NewLife Ltd, where she works as a scientist. The CEO of the Company, Professor Vladov, was also interviewed to give us his authoritative view on the finding. In our exclusive interviews printed below, you'll hear the story directly from the people involved.

"The significance of this event may take different shapes in the minds of different readers. Before you read on, I'd like to venture my hypothesis: with the two embryos showing this particular mutation, we may be witnessing, for the first time in history, human evolution at work.

"We know that microorganisms, like bacteria, but especially viruses, mutate frequently and may get, by chance, a new gene that confers resistance to drugs or jumps in species infection. Microbiologists have seen this often. But no one to date has witnessed in real-time a human genetic mutation that may confer an advantage. This is history in the making."

"Over, Ordi, now go ahead and add the interview."

I wonder what other scientists might think of this interpretation: a stretch, conjecture, speculation. It would be interesting to hear their comments. I think of Eve's parents.

Before leaving her in the Company's lab this morning, I put a note into her lab-coat pocket saying, *'Call your parents!'* Now I note a message from Eve on the e-mail window of my desk. I open it; it just says *'done'*. I decide to call her mother while I wait for Ordi to finish its job.

"Carol, how are you?"

She recognizes my voice instantly and sounds disappointed: "Oh, it's you."

"Carol, I am just about ready to go to print. The evening edition will be out by four o'clock and the radio interview on ABC News Drive at five-thirty. Do you want to get together for a touch of celebration later on?"

"Yes," Carol says, "we expect Eve this evening, at last, and I presume we might as well have the scoop winner around. Mark will be glad to see you. Does seven o'clock suit you?"

"Perfect. Looking forward to seeing you both."

I am not surprised at her bitterness and don't intend to react. Not now, not this evening. This is a great moment, also for me.

"How are you doing, Ordi?"

= WAITING ON YOU =

I check, reading slowly the interview. Ordi has misunderstood a couple of words from Professor Vladov. I correct them and give the signal to proceed. The layout is exactly what the editor wants.

"A final thing, Ordi. The full version you prepared is for the morning edition. You'll have to prepare a shorter version for this evening issue. This is to have the same intro, but only the first three Q&A of the interview."

Ordi shows on the screen the short version.

"Perfect, Ordi. Now the only thing left is to check if the 'crocodile' titled **Dilemmas of Embryos Implantation** is on page 2 of this evening edition."

=IT'S THERE =

"Let's close it, Ordi."

***

Five

With half an hour to spare, I decide to walk to Mark and Carol's place. Heading west from my house, I take a route with small buildings and ample space between them. The evening light has remnants of pink-orange hues; the air feels still soft for autumn. A few dogs barking tiredly and the odd car passing by don't make much noise. I perceive all this keenly: perhaps my generation will be the last to use senses naturally, unmediated by virtual contraptions.

Then I try an old game with myself: how long can I hold without a thought on my mind. I used to spin my head as a child to prolong that vacuum. Now it's harder. But the game is liberating, as always, and I arrive relaxed, it seems.

Mark greets me at the door with a strong shake of both hands on mine, his metal blue eyes under eyebrows lifted in the mid-forehead, expectantly. I see Carol behind him and hurry to kiss her on the left cheek as usual.

Her neck is stiff, unresponsive, as she says: "Eve is being delayed by a television crew but will be here soon."

I note she has cut her white hair even shorter.

Mark quickly asks: "Cinzano Bianco or Campari?"

It'll be Bianco; I need sweetness now.

We enter the family room that extends from the kitchen and opens onto the terrace at the same level as the garden and pool. We are going to sit outside, but only Mark comes out; Carol seems busy in the kitchen.

"Sorry, Mark, I haven't been in touch lately."

"Understandable." His reply is matter of fact, no emotion attached. Mark got a Ph.D in biochemistry and worked in biomedical research for a long time, at one stage together with Carol. Now he is an analyst for a major Biotech fund, selecting projects and companies to invest in. He has honed a skill that Carol lacks: putting himself in other people's places, trying to see other peoples' point of view. This makes it harder for him to confront the other. But I guess he wasn't aggressive to start with.

"How is work going, Mark?" I'm anxious to change subject.

"Quite well actually." He's relieved too. "This year Australia has reached the symbolic number of 500 Biotech companies, thanks to us too."

"Which are the areas of new growth?" I ask, putting on my recent news-seeking hat.

"Regenerative medicine by far, in all its supply-to-service chain: from robotics for stem cell production to clinics for cell transplantation, and in the middle, R&D companies working to discover new methods to grow, or to find new applications for stem cells."

"Has venture capital finally taken a liking to Biotech?" I ask ironically.

"You know," he smiles, "considering the risk that venture capitalists take now—compared with that taken by investment and other bankers in the sub-prime fiasco—it's a breeze. One can easily say that Biotech has behaved impeccably, and after all, in time, with success. The main reason for this is that the pharmaceutical industry is relying more and more on Biotech, which in a sense has given them a new direction."

"What do you mean by that?" I ask.

"Well, first you have pharmacogenomics, a whole new field invented by Biotech. With this, they have discovered that some people react one way to drugs, but differently from other people."

"And that is due to their genetic make-up."

"That's right. We knew that before, but now Biotech has given us the tools to predict from our genetic make up how we're going to react to a certain drug. This has been bad news for the giant pharmaceutical companies that relied on blockbuster drugs. They can't sell the same drug to everyone! The market is more segmented now. There is a bigger number of smaller drug markets, but at the same time, the new drugs are safer, with fewer side effects, because they are tailor made."

"I suppose there will be a rush to test one's genome," I say.

"Exactly. Gene diagnostics is going to grow enormously and that's good news for Biotech."

"And where does Biotech stand in regenerative medicine?" I ask.

"Well, the pharmaceutical industry had to let go of certain markets and Biotech stepped in. But that's not all; in fact things are pretty complicated."

"I could write articles on this."

"Come and see me in the office. I'd be glad to show you around and give you the full picture." He gets up. "I'll go and see if Carol needs help." He goes inside and leaves me in the company of their two Schnauzers.

I caress them while looking at the exotic mix of plants that grow in the spacious gardens. They reflect scientific knowledge of the terrain, but also, I suspect, the memories of their trips together, often to South East Asia.

Carol followed Mark's movements around the world for a while. Bern in Switzerland, then Boston gave her opportunities and her academic career took off as good work and luck propelled her into prestigious laboratories. Book chapters and 300 peer-reviewed articles published, medals and grants tripping over each other; she's had a great professional run.

Eve appears at the garden gate. She is showing off a bottle of Krug champagne. "Look what I got from Leo's fantastic cellar!"

"Is it chilled?" I ask.

"Just out of my cold packs."

I finish quickly my vermouth and wash my mouth with ice from the chiller. I stay outside as a schoolboy expelled from class, while the three of them greet, kiss and talk in the kitchen. Perhaps I shouldn't have come.

But Mark is now yelling, "Here we are!" as all three come outside carrying glasses, Krug, and finger food.

For a while there is cheer and humor, everyone wishing Eve good luck. Carol joins in. She is a tough but fair woman and she knows what is right. Her daughter stumbled on a scientific marvel, now she definitely needs good luck to take it through to a good outcome. Eve is clearly happy. To have her parents involved, almost on a par with her—she will tell me later—is a first. I've known for some time that she had a lot of discussions with them when she left academia to join a private company. They thought that her scholarly career was over, that she would become just a service provider, not a discovery scientist.

Even her father who, after all, had made a similar move, was opposed. He said his move was driven simply by financial motives: someone had to do it, but one's sacrifice seemed useless if it did not save the others from drifting out of pure science, for which Eve had shown enough talent.

We chat lightly as the Schnauzers jump up my legs and get some food.

"Eve, why didn't you tell us?" Carol says quite unexpectedly.

"I didn't tell anyone, not until the interview." Eve looks uncomfortable.

"And we are *just* anyone, are we?" Carol cannot hide a hurtful look.

"And you!" She turns quickly towards me, her voice sharp with anger. "Are you proud as ever to be her sole confidant?"

I know Carol well and choose not to answer.

"Are we ready for dinner?" Mark is standing up now and puts his hand on Carol's shoulder, giving her a quick, gentle stroke. Duty calling, she can't resist and moves towards the kitchen to fuss about the stove again.

The table has been set in the formal dining room. Is this to give importance to the occasion, I wonder, or Carol's way of showing some distance? Carol is busy with dinner and its many requirements. Her food is well prepared, impeccably served, and involves many variations.

She offers different sauces, perhaps more yoghurt, or gherkins? She seems to have contemplated the variability of individual tastes and covered all bases. This makes dinner a busy affair that involves Carol constantly, while Mark and Eve, impervious by habit to all this, chat away. I normally discuss variations with Carol, but tonight I don't dare and accept all offers from her, incompatible as they may be.

After dessert, when the little bottle of *Baume de Vènise* I had brought is sadly empty, Carol sits down, carefully placing her napkin back on the table. This is not a good sign, I think. We normally relax at this stage and have coffee in the lounge. But before I get signals from Mark or Eve, Carol begins.

"OK, let's see what we've got: a simple observation of a biological anomaly in two specimens. There are two possibilities: one, despite their unusual speed, these embryos are normal in every other way and may develop into perfectly healthy babies; two, they carry other genetically induced abnormalities that, if implanted, will lead them to abortion or worse, to strongly handicapped lives."

Her tone is acid and her voice, normally quite nasal, is increasingly strident as her argument moves towards the worst-case scenario. But the structure of her speech is not leading to condemnation; I know her well enough to think so. No, she is working her mind to solve potential problems; she is putting her highly honed scientific talent to Eve's task. She is critical, but she is using scientific criticism, which dissects first to eliminate dead ends in order to put together a new construct.

Eve and Mark wait, looking uncertain but not overly worried; they must have the same impression as mine.

"The problem here," Carol continues, "is that you have to work out at the molecular level all possible outcomes. You obviously can't conduct the experiments on the embryos themselves and no one will give you the license to proceed with implantation before all molecular mechanisms have been tested. An enormous task."

The conversation takes on the shape of a scientific seminar with the four of us engaged in detailed propositions on how to move next to prove what, to eliminate this, to experiment on that. I realize I am missing these mind storms, where targets, methods, tactics and strategies are worked out in parallel, at the same time with amazing speed. Different minds offering disparate elements that may be picked up or let drop, depending on the quick judgment of experienced brains. It gets heated but not offensive.

Eve has the advantage of a relatively recent but specialist knowledge of embryology. She has the confidence of youth that allows a greater scope of possibilities, higher inventiveness, and a good dose of optimism.

Carol's talent and experience are transportable. Her research on cancer happens to be very relevant to embryos. Tumors and embryos have in common a certain pattern of growth, with speed increased by the lack of dampening or terminating mechanisms. Tumors and embryos share certain active genes and both are programmed to grow fast.

Mark intervenes with his sharp analysis and a recently acquired skill for taking pathways through to their final conclusion. His new career requires him to test each route and discard the ones that have more than their fair share of obstacles, which happens very often with Biotech.

His biochemical background is very relevant to Eve's problems, since genetic mutations are eventually expressed in an altered or alternative biochemical pathway. The ability to follow this step by step with new biological probes will give Eve the tools she'll need in her investigations.

As for me, I think of just listening to the active scientists, but at some stage it becomes clear that some of my qualities might be useful in this discussion. My inclination to synthesize, rather than linger too long in technical details; my constant search for significance rather than method; both serve me well in this context. Others can dream up all the details; I jump over their shoulders and reach a faster conclusion.

At the end of the evening there is broad consensus about the road ahead. There should be two lines of investigation and two sets of parallel collaborations. One, to be explored with a Boston group that Carol knows, will follow the stem cells derived from the two embryos, and a number of specific tasks are mentioned.

The other would be done at Villejuif near Paris, if they agree, with the aim of a full genetic analysis of the two embryos, to try to anticipate their development and any possible problem with it. Much stronger on the back of her long experience, Carol will help Eve to write the proposals and to budget for them.

As we leave I realize that Carol is definitely hooked up.

"I could come to Boston with you, Eve, if we can organize the trip for sometime in September."

"Well, let's aim for that, then," Eve is quick to reply, though she looks surprised. Her mother is usually very busy. I feel I could go with her to Paris, where I have good contacts and know how to interpret the French mindset, but don't mention it yet—not here.

***

Six

Eve is driving me home after her parents' dinner. As she sits at the wheel, I can't help thinking of its symbolism: our roles have suddenly reversed. She is now in charge, the one who will lead this adventure. Her energy is palpable; a newfound confidence shows from every move she makes. Even her posture at the wheel makes a strong impression on me.

"How do you feel, Eve?" I ask, expecting a long answer.

"Elated, enthusiastic, energized. What more can I say? You know, I've had more time than anyone else to think about what happened. At one stage I asked myself why should an event like this, on which I had absolutely no influence and for which I can't claim any credit, propel me to fame. But that's what happened."

"Do you think you can stop the media calling? Do you want to?"

"I'll have to. Because I'd repeat the same things *ad nauseam,* but also, I don't have the time. Now that the news is out, I've got to prepare the proposals in detail for the overseas research; then talk with the embryos' parents, get up to speed for the ethical issues, and so on. I'll have very little time left for public appearances."

"What can I do to help?" I ask, with a weak feeling about my role.

"Can you interview the two couples, the embryos' parents? You have a knack for going to the heart of things with people. I've only had a passing contact with them. That's when Leo brought them into the lab, all masked and contained, to see their embryos. They were stunned at the thought that those blobs of a few cells were so special. And that's all they said."

"What about Leo? How is he treating you?"

"Oh," Eve pauses, taking some time before answering. "He's changed towards me. His manners have always been sort of lofty, you'd say elitist. In the past he's always been courteous, making sure he'd include my name in every speech he made when he talked about our work. So he's never been dismissive. But somehow he managed every single time to avoid talking to me personally.

"Now he comes to my lab, sits on a stool beside my bench and speaks to me, explaining in detail the aims of the Company, its plans for the future, the strategic mission and so on. Not just the usual pep talk I heard from him at public forums; this is much more personal, as if he was talking of the Company as a child of his."

"And what do you say then?"

"I just sit there and continue to work. He never asks questions. He seems to want simply to take me into his close circle by making me more familiar with the Company's history. And subtly taking care to suggest that I belong to the Company's next phase."

"Do you think Leo will support your proposals?"

"Oh yes, he said so. He's hinting at a maximum budget, a high six-figure sum, which he would support at Board level. A figure, I must say, that's beyond my wildest dream. So, we'll be able to afford international collaborations."

"Talking of cost, I'd be happy to chip in my own costs and time, if you wanted me to join you in Paris for the initial talks there," I say.

"That would be great! You know I don't speak good French, and their way of approaching scientific problems has always confused me. But I'm very keen on their collaboration. They've made real inroads in the genetics of embryos."

"I'd be glad to help," I confirm. "Of course, for a start, we'll have to talk to them from here, let them get the news and allow them to make the first move. They are very sensitive in that domain."

"Fine by me . . . ." Eve starts whistling *La vie en rose*, trying to mimic a jazz version with a particular riff. I wonder if she knows Jacques Loussier.

"What about Tim? Have you broken up then?" I say after a while.

"Well, that was my other big surprise, after Leo's." She giggles with a sense of satisfaction that is new to me.

"I asked to see him for lunch today, after we finished the interview and Leo had also gone. Tim didn't suspect anything until he saw your crew passing by the external corridor. He said he went to see Penelope to find out what was going on, but she was, as always, unhelpful."

"Of course."

"Then he queried our group in the Embryology Division, but all they could tell him about was my unusual working hours in the lab, my copying the lapsed photography on disks and my 'furtive' examination of a couple of embryos."

"You hadn't told your colleagues, anything at all?" I am surprised at her ability to keep this story to herself in a lab where things are done, shown and discussed with as many people as possible to get their comments, criticism and suggestions.

"Nothing, I'd said nothing, with the excuse that I wasn't sure, that I needed time. And of course they were all busy, you know, with their own searches, experiments, reports and so on."

"So what did Tim have to say when you told him?"

"He was taken aback at first; he was speechless. That gave me time to tell him all about the embryos, and especially the stem cells.

"I insisted on that and made some leading comments, practically asking for his help. So when I finished and he'd recovered from his surprise, Tim said he'd be glad to give us a hand. You know, that moved me really deep.

"So he gave me some ideas on how we could study the stem cells, those ideas that I talked about this evening at Mum and Dad's place. I think we'll involve him in the project. He has a lot to offer and his team will learn a great deal from us too."

"Would Leo like that to happen? I mean the collaboration."

"I think so. Remember when you questioned him on which application would be more time-efficient? He answered: the stem cells.

And I think he'd like to involve another group, not just mine, to spread the risk. He's right, of course. Tim's team is used to handling stem cells, analyzing their genetic characteristics and growing them in optimal conditions. They'd make the technical risk much smaller."

"What do you need the Americans for, then?"

"They are something else. The US group in Boston poached some of the best brains in stem cell research as soon as the Obama administration allowed funding for this kind of work in government laboratories."

"It had been outlawed by Bush, of course."

"Right. So big brains from Wisconsin, California, even Australia, came to join an existing group in Boston that was, until then, privately funded, and all were given brand new labs and major equipment in the Tuft University campus.

"Now they run the biggest stem cell research group in the world. You know how research has become big science. Well, it's really a matter of time efficiency, sharing expensive equipment, cross-fertilization and so on. With the Boston group, their robotic analytical system, their immense database, we'll get there much faster."

"So Tim is happy, Leo is happy, you're happy—"

She interrupts me. "Mum is happy! That was the biggest surprise. I felt so good tonight talking with her as a scientist, not just a restless daughter! You know, it's the first time this has ever happened." Her voice is raised; her pleasure seems unbound.

"Oh, I am not going to sleep tonight! Why should I? I probably won't feel this high ever again!" She stops in front of my house and quickly dials a number that lights up under the name 'Tim'.

I kiss her on the cheek and wave goodbye.

My wife's study has the lights still on. As I enter, I show little surprise. Being a corporate lawyer, she often works late at night.

"I heard your interview on radio," she says to my expectant look. "Excellent, your best to date. You went to the crux of the matter and it was very clear. I didn't know much of what you were talking about but

I think I understood; it's a big deal." She nods. "How did the dinner go?" Martina now seems unusually interested.

"Very well, in the end. At first there was some tension. You know Carol. She needed to let us know that Eve and I had behaved badly, excluding them from the news. But then she was caught up by her curiosity about things scientific, by her knack for fixing knowledge problems, and she was in. Now we'll all be involved in this project, I think. Perhaps I'll even try to pick your legal brain sometime."

"Perhaps tomorrow?" She closes her file, looks at me with a strange smile, and then switches off the lights.

***

Seven

Of the weeks that followed I have a troubled memory: a sense of anger, then dismay and disappointment. It's true that we had been naïve; perhaps we should have expected the reactions our going public would trigger.

But Eve didn't help. Confident as never before, she chose to dismiss public comments as background noise, nothing more. She had her parents helping to prepare the proposals for future research and Leo was only too happy to shield her from the media. She was now central to all decisions, but unavailable and protected.

I was instead thrown into the ring and was obliged to fend off criticism, to correct the record and keep the story on an even keel, all with my pen as the only tool. My weekly column was the pulpit, and for three weeks I chose no other topic to write about, with my editor increasingly annoyed by competitive press articles.

One Friday he summoned me into his office where he had prepared a collage of extracts from Australian online and printed articles—which he took care not to identify for some peculiar reason—with the first few sentences of each:

(Blog)

CARE FOR A BABY, QUICKLY?

You thought lab-coats had something better to do? Think again. This woman with a Petri dish just made embryos that grow so fast, she can snatch a full baby in six months! Do you want to know more? Read on.

(Morning Tabloid)

PREGNANCY CUT BY 3 MONTHS:
NO DISCOUNT

A Sydney researcher in a private company has managed to create test tube embryos with superior speed. You can get a baby in six months instead of nine, but don't expect a discount. The procedure will cost you over $19,000.

(Leftist Broadsheet)

GMOs ARE HUMAN

Genetic engineers, not content to manipulate cottonseeds or mouse ears, are now on to human genes. In an Australian laboratory, a private company scientist has managed to obtain human embryos that grow so fast they come to a full term pregnancy in only six months.

(Conservative Broadsheet)

IN VITRO FERTILIZATION LEADS TO ANOMALOUS
EMBRYOS

The practice of IVF, widespread in recent times, has finally shown its limitations with the finding yesterday of embryos, created in a private laboratory, so altered that they complete their fetal growth in only six months. The interventionist craving of certain 'progressive' forces, with their invidious wish to play God, has taken them too far this time: these babies may yet present serious abnormalities.

As I rolled my eyes, the editor promptly packed me off to work on a reply. I started by trying to correct the perception that the two anomalous embryos were the product of some manipulation on Eve's part. The blogs were driven to frenzy over 'Frankenstein babies'. Their idea was picked up by TV current affairs and by the last generation of conservative radio jocks.

The Catholic Church's spokespeople, too smart and well informed to believe in biological manipulation in this case, nevertheless treated the event opportunistically and renewed their attack on the practice of in vitro fertilization (IVF). The anti-genetic manipulation lobby then entered the fray, predicting the end of the world as we knew it if we persisted in altering the natural birth of living organisms. This was uncontrolled madness.

The fragmentation of my replies—one time to answer the moralists, another the doomsayers, yet another those who believed that it was all a conspiracy to extract more dollars from the Company's customers—all this made simple arguments impossible and complex reasoning too difficult to be effective.

Scared by the mêlée, the embryos' parents withdrew from view and refused interviews. My editor finally felt we had to come up with something more than my tired column, and one day he extracted a rabbit from his hat.

He said he would use his (reflected) influence to draw together a group of influential thinkers, people no one could suspect of conflicts of interest, to write a letter to our paper and clarify the essence of the matter. According to this scheme, we had to find at least six personalities, eminent people who had both the expertise and the conviction to lift the game and move it along. I passed the idea over to Eve, who asked Leo, who warned the e-parents.

Recharged, I helped my editor to select a number of personalities. They had to be above politics, unattached to medical enterprises, unaffected by personal circumstances, and in general not shy to come out with a definitive stance on the delicate subject. The editor made the introductions and I met them personally to discuss with them, one by one, the topic. From their answers and their availability, we selected 4 men and 2 women; all highly regarded as members of the influential elite we may call the intelligentsia.

One woman, the chancellor of a major university, agreed to draft the letter for the group. They went away and promised to provide the final piece in two weeks time. In that period, my column talked about anything but the embryos. The traffic on the blogs diminished and popular media stopped addressing the topic, except for referring indirectly to the 'biological wars' that had been lost by the 'manipulators'.

I was no longer attacked at dinner parties for being the major proponent of a faster, super race and my wife seemed to lose interest again. Then one day the eminent group's letter landed on my desk by registered, confidential mail; even encrypted, they obviously didn't trust the net.

The general tone of the letter was not scholarly, fortunately, but carried a strongly documentary vein. Not unduly long, still it contained the major arguments against the problematic points that had been raised. It started with a clear indication of intent:

"We, the under signatories, are concerned citizens who wish to redress the errors that appeared in the public record of discussions over the recent news about fast-growing embryos. Our case is based on evidence, not subjective opinions.

"Many public comments in the popular press have referred to the directed manipulation of embryos. We'll address this point first. In fact the two embryos were found to have an anomalous growth <u>without</u> any intervention by the scientist involved. Science currently does not know how to modify embryonic growth and accelerate it.

"The duration of embryonic growth is an evolutionary characteristic peculiar to each species. In relatively recent evolutionary times, human gestation reached a balance between the size of the neonate's head and the stage of brain development. This is a very delicate balance that no one would dare to try to modify. The idea that a scientist dared to modify this fine balance is science fiction.

"Most of the other comments were directly or indirectly opposed to the practice of creating embryos in the laboratory by in vitro fertilization (IVF). This procedure is legal and accepted by a large majority of the population, with an increased acceptance from 69% in 1982 to 86% in

2001. The legislative framework that governs this medical practice varies from country to country, but in Australia, and in most of the developed world, it is very stringent and protects the moral status of the embryo.

"That is, of course, the official lay position. Religious faiths have different views of IVF, with Jewish and Muslim laws permitting it, while among Christians, only the Catholic Church forbids it. Again this reflects a minority view, at least among the three monotheistic religions.

"It is important to note that in natural, unassisted fertilization, 50-70% of all embryos are miscarried. In IVF, this is less than 30%, provided the mother is 40 years or younger. These figures indicate greater care in IVF than in nature. This care is offered to infertile couples with a degree of professional ethics that should make Australia proud.

"We look forward to the day when scientists will find out the mechanism by which the two embryos changed their growth pattern. The science we support is all about discovery, not manipulation."

The letter with the six signatures was given great prominence in our online and paper outlets, and I must admit, at a considerable cost. But the effort paid off because the letter remained the last word in public on the matter, signifying a moral victory for our camp.

I even got a rare phone call from Eve.

"You've done a really good job, I'm told. I haven't read all those articles they say were vicious, but I liked the way the eminent group took up our defense. Now, are you still available to meet the e-parents?"

"Do you think it's a good idea, Eve, to make their views public?"

"No, no, I didn't mean that. But I'd like you to question them, with me, and try to find out what the two couples have in common. What it is that induced their embryos' growth to speed up."

***

Eight

23 August 2013. The patients' room, with its comfortable couches, all beige and light blue, must have some kind of insulation behind the fabric that covers the walls. It feels strangely silent, yet the room is close to the reception and front desk of the Company's offices.

I notice a sideboard with an espresso machine, cups and biscuits. Great! I had no time for breakfast this morning. We have to do this interview early to let the embryos' parents finish before nine o'clock. It's the couple that works in the currency derivatives market. They didn't seem to be prepared to miss any time at work for this interview, as important as it may be.

Eve told me about the kind of work they do, but I'll have to ask them more questions to understand the rhythm of their jobs, the pressure involved and their reactions to them. All this may have some bearing on the chemistry of their bodies and their germ line. Today I'm using both my scientific journalism and my background in neurology.

Eve enters the room. She is wearing a white lab coat and looks less sprightly than she's been lately. I don't need to ask; she gets to the point.

"I'm afraid I have bad news for the O'Loughlins: bad genetic results on all their other embryos."

"How many did you form in this cycle?"

"Five, which is average. So in the past two days, with the fast one stored away, we've tested the other four embryos. Well, sadly we found that all, except one, have chromosomal abnormalities and will have to be discarded. There's only one that seems normal, at least for now."

"Did they rely on these other embryos?"

"Oh yes, they did. Because if she can't be implanted with the fast growing one, or if that doesn't come to term, at least she might have had a better chance with the spare ones. But now there is only one spare left."

"Yet she could go through another cycle, couldn't she?" I venture.

"I'd hate to try. It's been so difficult! You see, he's got a sperm mobility problem, that's the main reason for his infertility. But with this level of embryo abnormality, there must be other problems."

"Do you intend to tell them now?" I am afraid this might have an effect on the interview.

"I'll wait until you are finished." Her pager rings. "They're here."

Eve makes the introductions. "I'd like you to meet Peter and Alysia O'Loughlin."

She is pretty and has a very attractive smile. Dressed severely in a dark suit, her curvy figure is still notable in a very tight skirt and a pink silk blouse. Her blond hair is tied up in a bun high on the neck and her brown eyes are warm.

Warmth is definitely lacking in Peter. His face is very tense and there's something animalistic in his pale grey eyes. He squeezes my hand with athletic strength, not even trying for a smile.

While I make coffee for everyone, Eve starts chatting away. After a minute or two, I hear her saying: "He's both a journalist and a neuroscientist, but will not publish anything unless you agree."

"Good," Peter says, "we don't want any publicity at this stage."

"As you know," Eve continues, "we'd like to ask you questions on your way of life and your habits to try to find out the possible causes, that is the conditions that could have induced your embryo to change its growth pattern. You need to be absolutely honest and trust me that it will all be very confidential. Do you understand?"

"Of course," says Peter.

"Sure," says Alysia.

"May I start with a question to you both?" I sip my last drop of coffee and continue:

"How old are you?" I know the answer from their file; just an icebreaker.

"I am twenty-eight," she says.

"And I'm thirty-four," he says.

The interview is recorded so I don't need to take notes, but I have a list of questions.

"Any particular genetic or chronic disease?"

"None," Alysia is very quick to announce.

"None other than my sperm mobility problem." Peter is already on edge.

"Peter, what sort of job do you do?" I ask, concentrating on him.

"I am a currency trader. Basically, I analyze all market conditions to come up with a certain dollar price. I also manage currency risk and end up structuring derivative products."

"Is it a job you do in a team?" I ask.

"No, it's mainly a solitary job: I have to sit for hours and focus on any relevant data that may have an impact on the currency, whether in terms of price or risk."

"What is the main difficulty in doing this?" I pursue.

"To keep cool, maintain an absolute clearness of mind, not letting any emotion cloud my judgment. But I seem to be able to do this well."

"Would you say you are a workaholic?" What a rhetorical question, damn!

"I am not sure about your definition, but I do work hard and long hours, with maximum concentration."

"What do you do to relax?"

"Tech gadgets and wine."

"Do you mean you relax with high tech gadgets?"

"That's right. I buy every new gadget on the market. Whether smart phones, music casters, photo cameras and so on. But I also like to have special wiring in my houses for music on tap: inbuilt speakers, home theatre, electronic controls everywhere. You name it, I've got it."

"Do you enjoy using them after buying?"

"Oh yes, but I like mainly to find them first, and understand how they work, so that I am ready for the next new thing."

"You said you also enjoy wine."

"May I?" Eve interjects. "Peter, do you use any electronic gadget near your groin?" She gestures the place she refers to.

"Yes, actually," Peter replies, "for a couple of years now I have been using a special phone with a largish screen, the size of a small laptop, but it's really a phone. I keep it on for many hours during the day for transmission of direct data to and from our Shanghai desk. With special software, it's more secure than the net and more exclusive.

"I keep it literally on my lap so no one else can see it and I can look all day long at its text messages at the same time as at the screen data in front of me on the desk."

That can't be very good for his sperm, I think.

"But you were asking me about the wine." Peter goes back to my earlier question.

"Yes," I say, "what sort of wine do you prefer and drink most?"

"Almost exclusively red. Grange Hermitage or Super Tuscan varieties, if I can. I have done a lot of research on wine, learnt how it's made, the various techniques that Australian winemakers use and the traditional methods of old European countries. I've tried thousands of them but now keep my drinking to those solid reds I prefer."

"Do you know what would be the concentration of flavonoids in those wines?" I am glad there is some chemistry here.

"There is flavonoid accumulation, especially in Merlot and Pinot Noir, but there are also stilbenes, which may have other beneficial effects."

I take a quick note for future searches and then continue. "Do they affect you at all. I mean, if you drink more than, say, 2 glasses in one evening?" I am trying to quantify his capacity to break down alcohol.

"Oh, I can drink a 750ml bottle without any notable effect and no hang-over." He looks at his wife to seek her view and she nods.

"Yes," she says, "Peter takes his wine with great ease and he never drinks to excess."

"Do you enjoy wine too?" I ask Alysia.

"Yes, especially the trips we take to try new varieties, say this year to the Barolo and Asti districts of Northern Italy, and to taste the newly released 7 year old Brunello di Montalcino in Tuscany. It's a lot of fun."

"How about your job, Alysia? What do you do?"

"I work in currency derivatives sale. I work mainly with clients. Mine is not an analytical job like Peter's. Others work out prices, risks and structures. I find and meet clients to explain and sell our financial products. Some are short-lived—they change all the time—and so my role is multi-tasked."

"What do you mean by that?" I find financial operations obscure.

"Well, I wish I had twelve eyes, twenty ears and four mouths. It's a very sensitive job. I have to be tuned into all sorts of messages from bosses, traders, markets, competitors and clients. I've got to be sure and calm under pressure, extremely disciplined and numerically fast. Fortunately, I graduated in mathematics at Uni."

"Do you find your job stressful?" I couldn't do it.

"It's challenging, but it's also fun. Often I take potential clients out to lunch; I choose top restaurants and enjoy fine food, good wine and all the attention. Most of my clients are boring bankers or fund managers, much older than me, but they're curious and enjoy a young woman's spark."

Peter is luckily busy with his phone, or perhaps it's a calculated move.

"And do you take alcohol well, Alysia?" I ask.

"Not as well as Peter, but you need to be professional about all that. You enjoy it, you fight the effects with willpower, and you always get up early in the morning, no matter how you feel."

"Will you do this for long?" I dare to ask, looking at her impeccable skin.

"Oh no. In fact, as soon as I'll have a baby, if I can do it, I'll change jobs. Couldn't do this for long anyway, but I also want to be a careful mother, particularly in the first two years."

"Now I have to ask both of you a more difficult question, but again, this will be confidential. It's just that we need to try to understand your habits."

"Sure," she says.

"Go ahead," he says.

"You two work under pressure, though with different aims, and perhaps you need some help to ease your cognitive flow or to intensify mental focus. Do you take any enhancing drugs?"

"I'm often tempted," Alysia quickly answers first, "but I've seen some bad examples in older people. In the 90s I was just a young girl when an uncle did take cocaine for a while and ended up in a heap. Then recently I met a bond trader who was on a brand of methylfemidate. That was *not* a good encounter!"

"I've got colleagues," Peter intervenes, "in the currency future exchange who've taken, at times, Modafinil to stay awake at night, but some come up with skin rashes and others become addicted.

"I've looked up the whole chapter and verse of cognitive enhancers and the conclusion I've drawn is that these drugs only benefit underperforming brains or brains affected by neurodegenerative disease. Do you agree?"

"Well, I couldn't be as categorical as you, Peter, because there are always new products on the market. But of course the very aim of those drugs is to help people who have problems with their mental health: a faulty memory, lack of focus, diminished planning or inept abstract reasoning, and so on. Such drugs were not developed to enhance normal brain function, although some people like to use them anyhow." I can exclude this couple from that category.

"Do you think we should know anything else about you?" Eve asks.

"Perhaps the fact that we never stop." Alysia's smile seems a little jaded now. "Our life is a storm of activities; sometimes it feels that, if we stopped, the world would fall around us."

"Yes. In fact we must move right now." Peter is up on his feet and gives her a hand. This line of thinking seems to embarrass him and he brusquely thanks me for the coffee before they start to walk out of the room.

But Alysia hesitates, then turns back to Eve with a timid look on her face and whispers gently before leaving, "Please take care of our little ones."

We are back on the couch, both looking and feeling fairly depressed.

"You didn't tell them," I say, referring to the other embryos.

"How could I?" Eve sits there for a while, while I pack my recorder. We haven't got a clue about the speed's cause; perhaps there is something there that will stand out when we compare it with the other couple's answers.

"When is the other couple coming back from LA?" I ask, knowing that they spend part of the Australian winter in athletic training there.

"Next week. I'll call you."

From her dry conversation, I reckon Eve is still thinking about those abnormal embryos and their demise. With only two left—one of which is a mutant—Eve's main purpose, a normal pregnancy for this couple, is not likely to be satisfied.

***

Nine

6 September 2013. It is a fine vantage point. I am happy to stand on the bridge to Balmoral Island, waiting for Eve and scanning the field. Looking southward on the high, dry side of the beach I see, among others, a young couple running with extreme ease, in fast strides tempered by a relaxed frame, yet maintaining a straight posture. Quite a professional display, I think.

"It's our couple all right." Eve smiles as she joins me—things must be going well in the lab. She waves and the couple wave back while approaching the bridge. They pass underneath and continue over Edwards Bay, leaving us behind to watch them. Running makes her long, dark ponytail swivel from left to right and back, like a single windscreen wiper. He sprints ahead of her for a while, then stops and waits.

"Do you want to find a quiet place on the island to sit and talk until they are finished?" Eve leads uphill. I follow.

Balmoral, home on and off for the past forty years, was a natural choice for me when the couple requested an open-air venue for our interview. Now, sitting on a rock at the top of the tiny island, I feel a familiar pleasure in looking over at North Head and the ocean beyond. I like to visualize those long waves slowly coming to rest on my beach.

"You know," Eve emerges from her own reveries, "my very first memory of playing on a beach is here, with your little Max. He must have been five or six, a year younger than me. I can recall it so well! Or was it a scene from a photo they showed me later?"

"It could be," I reflect, tempted to go on and explain.

"Anyway," Eve continues, "those were happy days! After Bern and Boston, this kind of beach was so good for us kids.

"We had the freedom, the space—oh yes, your place just across that small park on the border with the beach. It was great! And the sweet *cenci* your wife cooked in those days, I can still feel them, crunchy yet soft, melting in my mouth!

"Yes," I can't help adding, "*cenci* is still one of the very few things she can cook well. But let's talk about our young couple before they come up. Why did they resort to IVF?"

"She had very irregular periods. That's something common among women athletes. But she was a severe case, so we had to stimulate her cycle and then do an IVF, even though she's only twenty-five. He's twenty-seven.

"Oh, another thing: they are off to London on Monday after only a week in Australia to see their families. Did I tell you they've been selected for the Olympic teams? He'll run in the one hundred meters, she in the four hundred; they are both sprinters."

"Clearly our two couples have at least one thing in common," I say. "They are on the move all the time."

"Yes, we haven't noticed much else yet, so let's hope your interview today comes up with something new." Eve smiles again.

"The other interview was clearly too short." I sound defensive. "But Peter was so tense, he made me lose focus. Now I'd like to ask him some more questions. Do you think it's possible?"

"You know," Eve pauses for a moment, "at first Peter wanted to speak to us over the phone. I guess we could still do that if you think you need to."

"Let's see what comes up today and then we'll decide."

We hear some voices behind us and turn back.

"Here we are. Hi, I'm Pat Reis."

"And I am Jane."

We shake hands. They both seem happy and relaxed, confident, with a trustful look on their faces. In some ways they are similar:

both have dark hair and fair skin, greenish eyes deep in their sockets.

They sit on rocks near by and extract strange contraptions from their sports bags.

Once inflated with a small helium pump, those things turn out to be white cool packs in peculiar shapes that they wrap around their thighs and lower legs with rapid, experienced movements.

"These cool packs," Pat explains with an air of authority, "can help to reduce the chance of small muscle injuries and inflammation. They have similar effects to cold baths, but are more adjustable to individual needs, and of course they turn up to be more convenient in situations like this one."

"For sure." I try not to sound amused.

"On top of that," he continues undeterred, "the helium pumping expands the gas already inside the cool packs and puts a slight pressure on blood vessels which were dilated during training. So the recovery process is faster."

They drink water from their own containers while looking at Eve, who has brought a small basket of dry fruits and nuts. She unwraps the separate bags and offers them to the Reises. They accept with enthusiasm and prompt my first question:

"What type of diet do you follow?"

"Before answering that," Jane interjects, "let me ask you two if what we're doing here is in fact going to help you understand why our embryo is behaving so, so differently? In other words, are you trying to establish if *we are responsible*, somehow?"

She speaks very fast, though her tone is mild and controlled. The bright blue cap she is wearing now conveys a visual element that enhances her quick delivery. This distracts me, but Eve is ready.

"You see," she says in a gentle voice, "we need to find out what happened to your embryo before it became one, before fertilization. Why is it different from all the embryos our group has handled in the past twenty-five years? With the exception of only one other, as you know, that has exactly the same pattern of growth." She looks at them to make sure they understand, and then continues.

"If we are able to compare your genetics and lifestyle with those of that other couple, and can pinpoint certain similarities, we'll have a lead. This will be only the beginning of an explanation, but your help today could be very important to show the possible route to follow."

Jane nods and Pat concurs. "Where should we start?"

"Perhaps with your diet?" Following Eve's, my tone has become softer, less matter of fact. Of course biological matters are delicate, if personal, and shouldn't be treated simply as scientific phenomena. But human fragility is very important—I must keep this in mind—and my search for biological answers will have to become subtler.

"Our diet? That's Jane's territory," Pat concedes. "I follow her coaching when we receive advice from the Institute's nutritionists and I let her talk with them if there are discussions of studies coming up with new theories."

"Yes, he does that," Jane seems to be proud of the fact, "and of course I need to read a lot to be on top of all new trends, so that I know why they tell us to change our diet from time to time. And the info is so thick, sometimes I slow down my training regime to be on top of it all. But it's worth it, because it's not just mine, but also Pat's performance that's at stake."

I wonder if all the anxiety due to this effort may be linked to her fertility problem, and more to the point, on to their anomalous embryo. But I hear her continuing to talk at a breathtaking speed.

"You need to know that our diets are, of course, a bit different. Our metabolism is subject to variable effects of male and female hormones, our enzymes are in different quantities, our size and weight being different and so on." She seems to be quite realistic about that.

The recorder is fortunately on, for future reference, but I start taking notes of the crux of Jane's long sentences, on what I deem to be the meaning of the busy activity in her mind. I stop her at times to ask more or clarify something. It's a long, drawn-out process during which

Eve observes, while Pat explains some of Jane's points and reveals a few novel ones.

We talk for over an hour, occasionally moving from one spot to another, covering also the couple's training regimes and other lifestyle habits that may be relevant to our search. In the end, Eve closes on a positive note:

"By the way, your spare embryos are all genetically normal."

Jane closes her eyes while Pat, visibly moved, shakes Eve's hand.

The silence, once the couple has left, is eerie.

"Do you want to have lunch?" I ask Eve.

"Great idea!"

We decide to stay in the area and walk to Bathers' restaurant on The Esplanade, not far from the island.

"I've been *dying* to try Alex Herbert's new cuisine!!" Eve is chirpy now. "I heard she's trained directly with Carlo Petrini, you know, the Italian who founded the Slow Food movement. All ingredients are organic, produced in New South Wales, and very fresh."

We sit at a quiet corner table overlooking the beach, and straight away I start checking the main points of our interview with Jane and Pat.

"Let's just concentrate on the leads, on the answers that could point to a link between the two couples." I take out my notebook and start reading the comments I wrote down while they were talking.

But Eve wants to study the menu and eventually chooses for both—I'll soon find out—four delicious dishes. In the meantime, I continue to read my notes. I've selected 3 leads in my summary of Jane and Pat's answers.

"The first thing that strikes me is the frenetic rhythm of both women, despite their completely different lifestyles. Somehow this has to be significant." My voice has a turned down, conspiratorial sound.

"Maybe," Eve says loudly, as if to stop me,. "You mean that Jane's training, her complicated attempts to be an athlete and at the same time a helpful partner with her diet-managing role, all that puts her on the same level as Alysia who, after all, admitted that she never stops. True, those are incredibly fast ways to live. You know what I'd like to do? I'd like to run telomere tests on both."

"Why?" I had not thought of that.

"They have shown that these end-bits of the chromosomes become a little smaller with each cell division. So if their cell cycles are somewhat accelerated by their lifestyle, the telomeres on top of their chromosomes would be shorter than in women of their same age. But that's just one lead. What's the next one?"

"Their use of Ginseng. Pat said they use it from time to time and have done so to lift their energy, but also to strengthen their immune systems that may be affected by extreme exertion. I wonder if the other couple use Ginseng too, perhaps for other reasons."

"Should we call them?" In a few instants, Eve gets their phone number from the office. But Alysia's is on voice mail only. Eve tries Peter's and explains to him the reason for our call. He rings back after moving to a more private place.

"What is it that you want to ask?" His tone is less than friendly.

"Just one question this time, Peter." I try to control my voice but I hear it coming out glacially: "We need to know if by chance you and Alysia have been taking Ginseng, either in tablets or tea."

"As a matter of fact we have, for about three months in the period before the IVF." Peter sounds surprised. "Why do you ask?"

"It could be significant. But tell me, what was the reason for taking it?"

"Well, Alysia heard or read somewhere that Ginseng was traditionally used to improve fertility, so we started taking those tablets. Then we noticed that our libido was improved too, so we kept taking the tablets and also started drinking Ginseng tea. Anything wrong with that?"

"I don't know. We'll have to ask some expert on herbal medicine. That's all for now, Peter, but may I call you again when queries crop up?" I've managed to warm up my voice.

"Sure." Peter is gone.

"Interesting!" says Eve after hearing about Peter's answers. "We'll have fun exploring this angle. Though I don't know how we're going to do that."

"Of course we need to learn about Ginseng's many active ingredients. I haven't looked at pharmaceutical botany since my undergraduate days."

"Same here." Eve makes it sound like her university days were distant too. "OK, let's hear about your third lead."

"Alcohol," I say. "Pat talked about it, although Jane seemed keen to avoid the subject. My notes say that he is not a regular drinker: too concerned about his running performance. But he's admitted to binge drinking in non-racing periods or just after the races."

"Yes!" Eve is fully focused now. "Recent studies have shown that alcohol binges can affect sperm DNA badly. Of course sperm is formed anew constantly, unlike eggs, so it's more vulnerable to ingested toxics like alcohol, especially in large quantities."

"And we know already that Peter drinks a lot of red wine. That's a match." I'm rather satisfied with my three leads. At least we have some alternatives to offer the French group if they agree to work with Eve in the new study.

But Eve is not finished yet. "I have a fourth lead," she declares.

"Remember that Peter talked about his phone gadget, the one he keeps on his lap all the time while working at the desk? Well, did you notice Pat today? He had some things attached to both his thighs."

"Yes," I recall now. "In fact I saw him when he took off the cool packs. He dried himself, then Jane helped him tie up on the inside of his thighs what I thought were small chronometers." I had written no notes about it because we were leaving at that stage.

But Eve continues: "I asked Pat about those things while walking down from the island, and you were helping Jane carry her huge sports bag. Pat said that they were small transmitters of a particular radio wave frequency that's believed to stimulate muscle fibers. They're experimental prototypes that he's happy to try on. Still, who knows, those radio waves may have an effect on sperm DNA too."

"I am really impressed, Eve. Well done."

"Four leads, four leads!" She puts her hand over her mouth, trying to suppress an excited laughter as we walk out. We part soon after.

There is a fresh sea breeze outside but I can't breathe freely from it now. I sense my throat tightened by a new tension. I feel suddenly uneasy with Eve's project, for her teaming up with other eager scientists to explore the deep mechanisms they know about and find molecular answers to her embryo's phenomenon. I am out of that game now, and for all my journalistic pretensions, I don't even have a new story to tell yet.

***

Ten

5 November 2013. Champagne Beach, Island of Santo. The largest island in the Vanuatu archipelago, Santo is sparsely populated and still quite wild. On the beach, it's just Piero and me walking and touching the light waters that take their pale yellow color from the fine sands. There is no construction visible, no boats, just a timber shelter on the grass of a nearby park, dark green and thick vegetation everywhere else. It's very hot and I take a dive while Piero looks for some particular pebbles he wants to take home, which is on another bay some one hundred kilometers south.

On the way here, he showed me the vanilla and ginger plantations he set up over twenty years ago when he came all the way from Milan, initially on holiday. A trained chemist, he stayed on and, in time, built an extraction and packaging factory for ginger crystals and dried vanilla beans. His products are registered organic, praised for their aromas all over the world.

A few months ago, an Italian friend in Sydney gave me his ginger and vanilla beans and recommended Santo for my next holiday. This was easily arranged when I felt the need to take a break from work. It's now nearly two months since Eve went to the USA, first with her mother, Carol, followed by her boyfriend, Tim. They are now working at the Boston lab that specializes in stem cell research. Carol and Eve have sent occasional news, but nothing I could publish. Yet since the story broke early in the year, I haven't found any other topic that has absorbed me so much. I tried to extend my link to the subject by writing several essays (still not published) on different aspects of the phenomenon we came to consider so special.

I even wrote a fictional story about a fast-growing embryo that lost its rapidity gradually as he grew from a baby to a teenager, becoming slow to mature as if to compensate for his rapid embryonic development.

My wife said that I was becoming obsessive. She suggested a holiday in Europe, where she would have liked to go but was too busy to leave home. Santo sounded more attractive to me, empty and wild, another world altogether.

I found Piero an ideal host, clearly enjoying new company and eager to listen to stories from what he called 'the artificial world'. He let me stay in a bungalow that belonged to his brother, who lived in Milan and came only rarely to Santo. A place built on the cliffs of a quiet bay with a path leading directly to pristine water holes with submerged vegetation. On my first night there I felt intoxicated by the sense of being absolutely alone.

On Champagne Beach, Piero now calls me: "Is everything OK?"

I suspect he wants to go back, but I find it difficult to move. The waves have a hypnotizing effect on me; they grab all my attention and I caress them on the surface. A hand extracts me from the shallow waters and leads me gently to the beach. Piero sits down next to me and starts talking about his wife and young son who are now visiting her mother in America.

"You know, I'm used to be on my own, when they are away; that's when I find my real self again. Then I start missing them and can't wait for them to come back. But you, I guess, have a different life—hardly ever alone—that's why you find it so intoxicating here in the wilderness."

I am surprised at his comments but can't fault them.

"My own 'self' at the moment is preoccupied with a story that at home and work seems to have run its course, but not for me. So I can speak of it only to myself."

"Do you want to tell me?" Piero offers, while he prepares to leave. I follow, gathering quickly my towel, changing my wet costume and jumping in the front cabin of his small truck. He is amused and smiles encouragingly.

On the way back, as he drives slowly over unsealed roads, I tell him the story, a short version of it that has no regard for what I was and did before Eve's 'incident'.

A man of science himself, a chemist, Piero absorbs the facts quickly, finding questions for the holes I leave behind, stopping me to clarify, often anticipating the next episode. It takes only an hour for him to pack the essence of the story and file it away.

It's getting dark and Piero offers to cook dinner for us. We agree to meet at his house in one hour.

Under the shower I hear myself whistling, my head light as if liberated. Walking down the road leading to Piero's place, I meet a group of local Venui and smile at them. Do they speak English?

As I approach Piero's door, which is almost hidden by branches of different orchid plants, I hear Vivaldi's Venetian Concert playing. It sounds foreign in this exotic setting, yet somehow relevant to the complexity of the tropical vegetation, as intricate as music notes. I feel I am in the right place.

Piero has cooked rice with small local prawns, mango slices, and of course plenty of ginger. Dessert is custard cream with a strong vanilla flavour drowning some local black berries.

The dinner is candlelit but the walls of the room, made of rough timber, cannot reflect the light, which remains only at the centre of our table, darkness covering us from behind. Silver cutlery and fine china, crystal glasses and white muslin napkins create a civilized centre towards which Piero and I are attracted, forgetting for a while the dark, rough surroundings.

Can I keep a bright center in my mind, even if dark thoughts surround it? I wonder.

Piero seems to have heard me when he says, "Wilderness can be destructive, you know, unless you manage to keep a core of civilization always present in your mind; this has to maintain ranking and include higher notions, distant somewhat from immediate use, from primal needs."

Surprised by his insight, I tell him how I appreciate his wisdom and ask him the favor of listening to my story again in a new light.

He agrees readily, but asks, "Why are you so interested in this story?"

"I wonder myself."

"Do you see in it a particular significance?"

"I see in it a choice. As scientists, we usually face the need to prove a theory right or wrong. There is then an element of creativity, of course, in formulating and proving a possible theory, but that's never interested me. Here there's something out of the blue. Pure chance it happened to Eve, pure chance I got involved. Suddenly our task is to solve a living rebus."

"Still, your task is to resolve it. Where is the choice then?"

"You see, when scientists prove or disprove a theory, they look for truth, in a sense, for the rules of nature. Here we are confronted with an unruly reality, an exception to natural order.

"Eve and I happen to be the ones to have a choice, to decide whether to stick to conventional wisdom and consider these embryos abnormal, or to believe that they are exceptional, perhaps the forerunners of future humans."

"Do you think their abnormal growth is an evolutionary trait?"

"It could be. These two embryos are exceptional because they grow fast. But they could have had another mutation which gave them, say, telescopic vision. It doesn't matter. It is their improvement on the norm, the leap forward if you like, that interests me."

"I see," Piero looks at me absently for a moment, "but I don't believe it's your choice. You've got to try and find out what is the underlying genetic change in these embryos and if possible, what caused it. But after all, it's the parents who will have the choice to bring their embryos to term, out in this world, or not."

"Of course. Still, Eve has control over them. She can decide to stop their growth—if we consider them abnormal—and terminate them . . . and I'd have a role in this decision." I lower my eyes as I say this.

"That would be a very strange decision," Piero murmurs, "and one that could have serious consequences."

He brings me back to a more pedestrian reality.

"I suppose I'm worried about Eve, but also about the project."

"Have you got news from her?" Piero asks.

"Yes, I get messages almost daily on my satellite iphone."

"So what are they doing now?" Piero seems eager.

"Well, the American collaborators want to take it step by step in due time. They intend to analyze the fast-growing stem cells, starting from their genetic material, to find out why their growth is so extraordinary, but also why they turn cancerous so consistently. In other words, they want to sequence the whole genome of these stem cells first. Then they want to compare them to other, ordinary embryonic stem cells to see if they're different. In short, the Americans have a systematic approach that Eve finds too slow for her liking."

"Well, what else can she do but agree?" Piero can't see the problem. Time, for him, obviously has a different meaning.

"What do you want to do when she comes back?"

"There is another aspect of the project that we could start considering," I say, touched by Piero's quick understanding of my psychology. "Eve is supposed to start a separate project with a French group in the New Year, but we still have to work out the details with them."

"What keeps you from starting?"

"Nothing really, just waiting for Eve." It now seems obvious that talks can start at any stage, especially since they will be done from a distance. It doesn't really matter if Eve is in Sydney or in Boston.

Back in the bungalow, I send a message to Eve:

"Let's move on the French negotiations. What are your minimum requirements?"

Her answer comes in after only a few minutes:

"Oh yes, please! Can't bear to wait much longer. I want control of timing in France, and with their help, a primary role in experiments. Tell them I'd bring the last two twins of my embryos; I have to leave the originals in

Sydney. I trust the French with experimental protocols; they know better than me what's needed to test embryos. Ask them also about costs. I'll have my expenses covered, but do they need funds from us for their testing?"

I put together a long message in French to send to Villejuif. They are much more formal than us. Just the greetings cover two lines. French is much less direct than English but I find it very suitable for negotiations. It takes a week before I have a clear understanding of what they want. I have plenty of time to go swimming, writing, and catching my own fish. I see Piero for a few minutes in the factory, to get fresh supplies, but leave him alone at night, get back to the bungalow and cook a quick dinner for myself.

The French now say that they will cover their own costs. They will add Eve's project to their current programs, which is allowed by their status as public service researchers. They reckon it won't take too long since they have plenty of staff and several projects that could easily incorporate Eve's.

They test embryos all the time; these two will form a class apart, but will undergo the same experimental protocol. However to do this, they will need to take ownership of Eve's two embryos; in other words, they need to buy them, otherwise they will not be allowed to use them. French researchers are under strict instructions. Property of the biological material they use is considered essential and is defined in unequivocal terms; it's either purchased or originated in house.

This might cause a problem, I reply, as Eve will not be able to sell the embryos. After several days, the French come up with an administrative solution that may solve the problem. There would be internal paperwork covering Eve's sale of the embryos on one side and her purchase of the French researchers' time on the other, the two squaring off exactly. This would be set in confidential documentation that would not be disclosed to outsiders. The only requirement would be for Eve to sign off on behalf of her Company.

I have qualms about this, but send their message to Eve nonetheless, making sure I don't hint either acceptance or refusal.

"No problem," replies Eve. *"I've already obtained authority to sign on behalf of the Company, not restricted to the American collaboration. It covers all international projects. Tell the French that I accept. They can draft the document and send it to Sydney. I'll be there in a week. Tim will stay in Boston until late December to follow the stem cell characterization."*

Eve is obviously more adventurous than I am. I feel a sting of bruised pride, but also relief that the project will not be delayed by the French request.

I send a message to Villejuif, relaying Eve's answer, but I also suggest that the agreement on this collaboration be drafted in a way that the word 'sale' doesn't appear and a euphemism be used instead.

This is no problem for the French, who send me various alternatives. We agree on a version that requires 'all materials used in the experimentation to be French, whatever their original source'.

The statement seems equivocal in English, but in French it sounds plausible.

This leads to the joint decision, checked with Eve, that the documents covering the agreement will be in French only and that I will be a joint signatory, once approved by the Company.

Eve is certain that I'll be given that authority. She assures me of Leo's eagerness to go ahead with the French project, especially since the American research, which costs a bundle, is not going that well at the moment.

She adds an interesting note on Leo's new thinking. Eager as he is to know the final results of the embryos' tests, he's distanced himself from her collaborative projects and stated that he'll leave to Eve responsibility for any potential problems that might arise from them.

Suddenly I feel the need to consult my wife, but I fear her reaction since she'd put on the lawyer's hat. I send her a few messages and explain the general thrust of the French agreement.

"You know I don't understand the French," she replies, *"so I won't be able to advise you."* Martina must be very busy, I think, or perhaps, like Leo, she doesn't want to be involved in this matter.

I decide to leave two days later and invite Piero to dinner on the night before I leave. I have caught quite a few crayfish harboring in the underwater vegetation of my little bay, patiently plucking them from the waterlogged leaves and collecting them in a fishnet.

With flour, eggs and water, I knead, roll and flatten fresh pasta, cutting it roughly in squares and making ravioli filled with crayfish meat, mixed with the fresh herbs Piero gave me yesterday. I cook a simple tomato sauce with just a hint of garlic, adding a touch of sugar to neutralize the acidity.

Dessert will be a gelato; I discovered that Piero's brother had brought an electric gelato machine from Milan. I've tried it a few times in the past two weeks, with mangoes, mint and mandarins. For tonight it will be a passionfruit semifreddo.

The evening is very still. We eat outside on the veranda overlooking the little bay. The candles are bright but tonight the moon makes a grand appearance: it's her show.

Piero and I talk about many things, scattering here and there our thoughts, that tonight don't seem to connect. We stop often and leave long gaps.

In that eerie silence a feeling of inevitability washes up on my mind. I arrived in Santo keen on a tropical holiday, intent on distancing myself from my obsession, hoping to resolve my status in a vicarious project.

Yet I managed to change only one thing: my activity is now less vicarious. I have negotiated a deal that I'm going to sign. I'll be directly involved in this quest to find out, or at least I'll be close to the action. No longer sitting and waiting to hear news from afar, I'll be there, ready to pick it up.

Moonlight shines on my plan and now that it is settled, I'm ready to leave this wilderness. Piero looks at me silently. He must have guessed that much.

***

Eleven

22 January 2014. *"At Sydney Airport on Saturday!"* Eve spread the news of our taking off for Paris. *"We'll fly Qatar,"* was the only other clue.

My wife, Martina, is here, Carol and Mark too. Tim arrives late and joins us in the external lounge. Now Eve is surrounded; that's the way she likes it. She begins to calm down. They all have some advice for me—recommendations that they know Eve wouldn't want to hear. They plead with me: be in touch often and don't spare us news, even the most trivial.

Carol takes me aside, whispering a secret about Eve's mental state. I had suspected something was not quite right, but didn't imagine this. In Boston a psychiatrist friend of hers has made a provisional diagnosis: anxiety and depression combined, a difficult condition to treat. I'll have to watch her.

Eve sits there sipping a drink, biting some savories. She is holding tight the handles of a special bag, the purpose-built transport container for the embryos. I know it has multiple layers inside and a liquid nitrogen-filled core that bathes the two dormant embryos.

The bag carries on top a special document from the Federal Police, which authorizes its export and states that the seal should not be broken. We have a similar document from the French Border Police for its entry into France.

I seem to have thought of everything and feel quite relaxed, then Leo enters the lounge and proceeds towards us.

"Great of you to come!" Eve is clearly excited at the fact that Leo has shown up.

"Well, I couldn't miss your departure, dear Eve." Professor Vladov greets everyone, then turns back to Eve. "I can't say I was amused to find out that you haven't yet identified the original two embryos in their canisters at the lab. Is that because, in all your excitement, you've forgotten the rules? Let me remind you that these are statutory rules, not just the Company's. You must know that our license could be in trouble. Imagine if an inspector visited the lab while you're away. We've been lucky it didn't happen when you were in Boston, but can't always rely on our luck."

Eve looks indifferently at him now, as if he no longer mattered, but takes her *G4ipad* from her handbag, touches various spots and comes up with 9F and 9J. Leo scribbles the two codes on his smart phone, smiles, and proffers a few more words of farewell before leaving.

I see Tim moving his mouth silently, repeating the codes a few times, and wonder why. Eve is still looking at Leo leaving. The others seem not to have noticed.

I approach Tim and quietly ask him: "Why do you need to memorize the code?"

He does not answer and shrugs his shoulders.

"Do you intend to go behind Leo's back?" I insist.

"Suspicious mind, I see. Well, help yourself. But what if Leo loses the code, or doesn't record it for some reason?" He grins and joins Eve, his arms opening and closing around her.

Leo's appearance has somewhat spoilt our happy mood, but we have no time to regain it. Our flight is called. We have to go.

The flight is uneventful: just one stopover in the Middle East, the comfort of advanced business class, and very little talk between Eve and me. We probably said all there was to be said in the two months before this trip, discussing alternatives, anticipating the French set-up, clarifying our respective roles. It is clear that Eve wants to work in the laboratory. I will be available for discussions, meetings and other joint exercises where my interpreting may be useful. I'll also write a diary of the events, as relayed by Eve or any other participant, and publish an article when I am allowed.

Arriving in Paris at Terminal 1 of Charles de Gaulle Airport, as agreed, we meet a young scientist, Luc. He is, in a sense, our guarantor and very quickly resolves all our immigration issues.

We have selected our hotel in *Rue du Bac* in the VI *Arrondissement*, where I used to live in the 90s. Small, smart rooms decorated in 2nd Empire style will remind us of the grand French past. Eve tells me that her parents have taken her to similar places to stay when visiting Paris a decade earlier, a pleasant memory, all in all.

Tiredness after the trip doesn't prevent us from sitting down for coffee with Luc, a good-looking, mild guy who clearly has an eye for Eve.

"*Mademoiselle*, I am so very happy that you are here. *Quelle surprise,* you are beautiful!"

"Well, you too!" Eve is clearly embarassed and doesn't quite know what to say.

"OK," I intervene. "I'm sure you'll have many chats like this in the lab, but we are tired. Let's be practical now. Luc, can you tell Eve how does it all work?"

Luc quickly explains the ways of his lab, including the complex hierarchy of those working in it and the rules of how to address them.

"Eve," he says, "we normally use '*vous*' or '*tu*', depending on rank and familiarity. *Bien sure* you speak English, so you can just use 'you' with everyone. But you need to say '*Monsieur*' or '*Madame*' and then the title. Just follow the way we do it in French: '*Oui, Madame le Directeur.*' You'll see; it is easy. Just do not use first names."

"But may I call you Luc?" Eve asks anxiously.

"Yes, I'll be working for you, so it's OK. Well, I'll let you have some rest." Luc gets up, flashes a splendid smile at Eve, and leaves.

Villejuif has an enormous hospital and medical research complex outside Paris and the following Monday we take in all its grandeur at once. "It makes us feel not just alien, but small and irrelevant," says Eve, "as if reminding us that they don't need you."

The lab where Eve will work is a pleasant place, perhaps smaller than I imagined, but well equipped. The first thing the secretary takes care of is a formal act where the embryos in their container change hands and both parties, including me, sign a document in front of a recording camera.

Eve and I are then escorted to a meeting room where we are introduced to *Madame le Directeur*, a dry, tall woman who tells us, in English, what we can expect. She uses the word 'must' very often, mostly followed by 'not'. There are clear boundaries here, Eve is inescapably warned. She seems deflated at the thought of having her initiatives curbed, but asks no questions.

"*Madame, puis-je?*" I start.

"*Je vous en prie, Monsieur, en Anglais.*"

I express, in English, my best wishes that the project may be of mutual benefit and continue with a direct request that Eve be allowed a certain freedom of movement in the labs.

"There will be only one lab for *Mademoiselle,*" the Director says firmly. "She will not be allowed in any other, except for the *salle à manger,* of course."

At least she won't starve. Eve will be given, the Director continues, a protocol with a list of duties and codes, plus the experimental plan that has been devised to test the embryos. Luc and a senior scientist, Gabriel Pons, will work with Eve and hopefully bring the project to fruition.

I ask if the results will be immediately available and the lady replies with a dry *non*. She explains that only the full set of tests will be able to give a meaningful answer to our question: what is the extent of abnormality in the two embryos? But, she adds, it will not take more than a month.

Eve has still a blank look on her face, seemingly resigned to follow the rules, but knowing her, I have my doubts. I am also wondering if I should stay here for the whole month; my plan was for a ten-day trip.

Madame le Directeur escorts us to the lift. Eve goes back to the lab while I leave the building/ It's all quite oppressive really. I return to Paris by train and distract myself by visiting new places, like the Greater Paris' Tour First at *La Défense*.

The business district has been enlarged with the construction of new skyscrapers which are really elegant, but still give me a sense of walking inside a maquette, the model architects build to show their design. I don't seem to recall the joy I used to feel when going around the traps in Paris during the 90s.

That evening I take Eve to a special dinner at *Le Procope*. Two months ago I made an online reservation to the restaurant that is still a legend after more than 200 years. Revolutionary ideals and literary fame may arouse Eve's spirits and mine, I hope.

On line, I also placed my order: Black Beluga caviar and the special, small galettes containing the exotic seeds that enhance the eggs' taste, with a 1996 Dom Pérignon grand cru; roasted pheasant and wild mushrooms with a Château Margaux 1982; a chocolat Éclair with Grand Marnier.

As we sit in the formal, dark room on the first floor, Eve asks an impertinent question: "Is your wife paying for all this?" She laughs.

"It depends. If you are referring to our credit card bill, I'd say yes. If you consider all our assets, my inheritance has covered them twice over."

"Great," she says. "It feels better to know it's not another woman's money I'm eating." She starts sipping her Dom with gusto.

The evening turns out so easy; it has the quality of a dream. The food, the drinks, Eve's behavior are all so perfect. We talk lightly for hours, mostly about history and its upheavals.

Towards the end of the evening, Eve is a little tipsy when she asks me, "What is sex for you?"

"A biological function, of course. Why do you ask?"

"You know how much I care about the two embryos; lately they've been the centre of my world. Well, today, working with Luc in the lab, I couldn't think of anything else than to have sex with him!" She laughs, positively excited.

"Go for it then," I hear myself saying. "It'll do you good."

She has a vaguely anxious look on her face when she says, "Don't you think it may interfere with the project?"

"I don't think so. On the contrary, it may give your work some extra spark. After all, this is going to last only a month. Ideal for a purely sexual affair."

During the following week Eve doesn't show up at our hotel. On the phone, she tells me that she is staying with Luc, who lives closer to Villejuif. I have time to revisit the sites I love in Paris: *Place des Vosges*, where I spent my first afternoon in France; *Montmartre*, descending from the Basilica's steps with colleagues after attending a neurology conference; *Notre-Dame*, where we heard a baroque concert after another international conference; Champs-Élysées at the parade for the 14th of July and then, at the end of that month, with an Australian friend, at the arrival of the *Tour de France*; a shoe shop near the *Arc de Triomphe* where my wife bought a pair of green suede shoes that she still wears.

After a week I realize that I am revisiting my memories, more than anything else, and decide to leave on schedule. I call Eve and ask her to organize a meeting with her group to work out the main current issues and write an interim report.

As she meets me at the lab, I notice changes in her demeanor. She seems more mature, a little distant, like her mother, but has a look of disproportionate anxiety on her face when saying, "There'll be just four of us, with Luc and Gabriel. *Le Directeur* couldn't make it."

We meet the others in a small lounge next door.

"How is it going?" I ask.

"Very well," says Gabriel. "We have been able to extract viable cells from both embryos without damaging them."

"Congratulations!" I knew it was possible, but this is real.

"And we've started the genetic tests. It will take several weeks to complete them, but we know already that they have no gross abnormality. There is no visible change at the chromosome level."

"You know," Eve interjects, "I've got news from Sydney."

"And?" I am keen to know that side of the story too.

"Well, the telomere tests on the two 'mothers' have come up with interesting results. They show a greater cell division rate when compared to their same age groups."

'Which means," I interrupt, anxious to show I understand, "that the telomeres on their chromosomes are shorter than expected, and that their cell division tempos have been faster than normal."

"Right, and that can be due, perhaps, to a genetic predisposition, or as you suspected, to their frantic lifestyle." Eve is in generous mood.

"And the 'fathers'?"

"Nothing. They found no abnormality in the fathers' chromosomes but their sperm samples have shown great variation."

"Meaning?" I ask.

"Well, something is going on in there, but it's difficult to pinpoint because the samples are, in fact, so variable. They change a lot from time to time."

"Could it be because of the men's alcohol intake?"

"Could be that, or the Ginseng, or some electronic gadget. We don't know."

"What can they do to find out?" I insist.

'To know for sure, we'd need quite a long trial, say on young, healthy students, looking for the effects of each of the candidate substances, plus tests of several men with similar work habits to our two. It would take such a long time, it's not feasible."

"And in Boston? Have they finished the work on the stem cells taken from our two embryos?"

"Yes, they have. There is a paper coming out with that study, where my name and Tim's appear." Eve seems to attach more importance to the publication itself than to the results.

"And?"

"They found that the stem cells, those that we treated with a particular methylating agent, have a much better profile. They differentiate well, after a large expansion in numbers, and don't seem to convert to tumors. So, all in all, that part of our project was successful in the end."

"And what are you working on at the moment?" I ask.

"We are trying to select and test a reasonable number of genes that, in the embryos, may be linked to their fast growth. There may be hundreds of them but we need to rank them in priority, since it takes time to analyze each one."

"Is this work you do under Gabriel's supervision?" It seems to me that she is taking too much credit for what they are doing.

"Of course. Gabriel has put together a large database of embryonic genes and their variations. We have to test our embryos' genes and then compare them to Gabriel's data."

"We need to know," Gabriel is back on, "to what extent these two embryos are abnormal. That is, what else do they have that could be classified as anomalous, like their growth pattern. *Vous voyez,* if their strange growth is due to a single mutant gene, that would be great! It could be modified back to normal and the embryos could be implanted like any other. But if they carry many abnormal genes, *non, ca ne va pas.*"

I take notes, careful to add a few explanatory words as they come to mind. I am hoping to write an article for my column on my way back to Sydney.

"So you are leaving on Wednesday," says Eve.

'Yes, and I think we should both leave the hotel. Do you agree?"

"OK, I'll be there to pick up my stuff on Tuesday evening. We could have a farewell dinner, but in a *bistrot* this time, *je t'invite!*"

Coming down the hotel staircase on Tuesday evening, I notice in the hall a pair of elegant shoes, a delicate floral dress and brown hair loosely knotted in a bun. Can't be Eve, I think, but it is, changed by Paris in a week, from a jeans-jumper-Reebock-boots-scientist to a very feminine sort of woman.

Changed by Paris or by Luc? I think of her strong will in the past to refuse any attempt of 'feminization' by her mother. Their discussions around the dinner table over the symbolism of floral dresses could lead to graphic descriptions of male behavior and its ultimate goal. But here she is, looking very nice and comfortable in one of those very dresses.

I hold my compliments—she is already aware of her newfound *charme*—and propose a bistro on the Rue Dauphine, one I frequented in the past. The timber top and metal frame square tables are the same, the wall still covered by the old photographs with Paris scenes of the early 20ᵗʰ Century. Everything seems to have retained the old character.

Except of course for the staff: a mix of North African boys and Eastern European girls attend the tables with less skill (and probably less pay) than the middle-age French men of my time.

I try to find our table near the western window: it's free. Eve sits down in the middle of a sentence, about which I hear only the word 'affordable'.

The menu is basic, but I notice on the opposite side of the room a new pizza oven with wood flaming. A young Moroccan-looking man is turning pizza dough in the air, attracting my choice.

Eve follows.

"Pizza likes beer," I say.

Eve agrees.

"Well, you look sharp and happy." I decide to get the compliment out of the way, since it's clear Eve is expecting it.

"Happy is an understatement," she says, "and a total surprise. I thought I'd resent the close quarters, having to work elbow to elbow with others, not having any freedom to go somewhere else."

"Quite unlike your large lab back in Sydney."

"Exactly. But in fact, the small space forces on you a discipline that doesn't allow any sloppy movement, as no mistake is overlooked; it pushes you to pay much more attention to what you're doing, no room for error. In the end I get quite worked up in a strange tension that seems anger to me until we arrive home and make love and I realize that's what it is."

"Satisfying?" I mutter, embarrassed at the topic. I've never talked about this with young people, including my own daughter.

"Fantastic! And if you want, I'll tell you, but you'd be uneasy, I know. Let's say that it's not like doing it with the 'Anglo-Saxon' men of the lab or the pub, one way only and quick.

"With Luc, it's a long trip for two and a lot of deep, deep lust! Then, after sex, love sets in so powerful and new that I could never imagine I was capable of that."

The evening concludes early, after the fruit salad, and it's Eve's turn to wish me *bon voyage*, see you in a month or so.

I've lost her. This is the sense I make of my bad temper on the way home. The plane is half empty and I request a change of seat, treating the hostess badly. I get what I want and soon am able to recline my seat and think.

Yes, I've lost her. But did I ever have her? I shared her mind; that's what I wanted, nothing else. Eve's thoughts were constantly open to me in a clear and pliable way. She was influenced by my words over the years and she also influenced my own thinking, our two minds mixing and exchanging ideas. Our mental connection was, I am sure, of a kind that was superior to any other.

Now that link is one of many, its ranking gone down at least one, if not two notches. What is disturbing is the loss of the special priority she once gave to intellect. Now sensuality prevails and what hurts me most is the satisfaction it gives her.

I know it's natural for a young woman to feel that way and I expect this to be a temporary state of affairs. But the memory of her greatest, sensual satisfaction will linger. Later, as she might want to go back to a more intellectual life, it will be too late to revive our exclusive understanding.

***

Twelve

After arriving back in Sydney, I waste no time and put together an article for my column, indulging in the subject that, in my mind, is paramount.

FAST EMBRYOS, A PROGRESS REPORT

Our embryos have traveled. Their stem cells have been to the USA, their twins are in Paris, and I am now back to report on their well-being. The American group, together with our Australian scientists Eve Latimar and Tim James, have managed to create an enormous, viable and normal pool of stem cells that will be used for the regeneration of diseased organs.

It wasn't easy, because at first it seemed that these cells could change to the point of producing cancer. But the scientists worked hard to find a chemical solution that allowed them to grow and reproduce large numbers of stem cells without the risk of cancer.

Now the few stem cells, that were originally part of our two fast embryos, have become billions and will soon be implanted to regenerate heart muscles, brain connections, joint ligaments, and many more. Some of them will return to Australia soon to be part of our own organ regeneration pool.

What about the twins? In Paris, where our Eve is working with a team of experts on the genetics of embryos, they have found out a few preliminary things. The embryos have no major genetic abnormality. At first glance they appear normal to the experts. But the fine comb has yet to be applied.

Even if the embryos have the normal number of 23 chromosome pairs—by the way, they are both males, so the 23rd are both Ys—even if all chromosomes appear intact under the microscope, they might still carry genes that are not altogether normal. And that's why the scientists are applying their fine combs to the next level down, to the genes themselves. Do these embryos' genes carry any abnormal variation? One that prevents them from exerting their function in a normal way?

Each function is a set of steps in a biochemical cascade where one misstep could cause the breaking down of an important biological activity, like the variation found in hemophiliacs whose blood cannot clot normally and who can bleed to death at their first cut.

And then there is the possibility that the genes might be entirely normal, but they can't be expressed in a normal way. Looking, say, at two single genes for testing their expression: is one on and the other off when they should be one off and the other on? This is tricky stuff that requires a lot of time to be tested. So we don't have all the answers yet, but so far so good.

The embryos' parents are holding up well. Their life has changed somewhat though. They are now not altogether able to decide for themselves what to do next. For months their decision about whether or not to have babies has been, and is, on hold. Their anonymity broken, they are now not just themselves, but also the e-parents, a connotation that makes both temporarily suspended in limbo—or dare I say, in liquid nitrogen—and dangerously on edge. They are nevertheless still trying to lead a normal life and have declined any offer to be interviewed. But they may one day talk to us, if things go well. Stay tuned.

I've just finished dictating my article to Ordi when I notice a message from Eve: "Had a good trip back? Do keep in touch."

As soon as Ordi puts it into the system, I send her the article with a few words on my trip: nothing too personal.

We start an exchange of messages that, almost daily, keeps our correspondence going, with Eve providing the subject matter—her experiments, her results, her criticism of the French.

From her messages I slowly stitch together a new view of her scientific life, perhaps one that she had all along but was too inhibited (by me) to express; perhaps one to which Luc and Gabriel are contributing.

"Have you reflected much on the limitations of what we know?" she wrote once.

"We get greatly excited when an experiment seems to work, when we have a result that makes sense. We then try to put that into context, in the big framework that thousands of other scientists have contributed to build. Yet all that construction is so fragile that a mistake, or another experiment contradicting our house of cards, can bring everything down in a heap."

"What happened to the ideal of building knowledge on the shoulders of giants?" I ask her in reply. "What of patience in building and rebuilding theories until they are solid and safe? What of the pushing forward, following chance, of new realities, like our exceptional embryos?"

"Yes, à propos of our embryos," she replies, "they are our exception, all right. Perhaps they represent something of the future, where most human populations will have exactly the same mutation.

"But now we happen to have only two. Hardly the start of a population. We are the ephemeral witnesses of a phenomenon that might take thousands of years to adapt and spread widely. We have been given a taste of the future to which we don't belong. What's the use of it? How are we going to live after tasting the future?"

This is not a question I can answer.

A week-long silence follows, during which I try very hard to get interested in some other topic.

Then another glib message:

"You know, my parents were right. I shouldn't have left pure science. Working here, I realize that I can still function perfectly in the lab but during seminars, when people discuss their research, I am stultified. I can't make the leap from minute results to the main framework all the time. I'm stuck in micro-management when I should juggle micro and macro at the same time. And it's not the language: there are many international students here, so most discussions are in English. In fact, I should be advantaged. My parents were right, I shouldn't have left academia, but I didn't see the point then."

What role did I have in that decision? I can't remember.

Then, a few days later, Eve sends another depressing message:

"I didn't know that Luc had applied for a scholarship in the USA, but he's got one to do a PhD at the NIH near Washington. He could have done this in Australia. He'll leave in two weeks. And you know what he told me? That he was very grateful for my constant application of English; he said the past month was like a total immersion language course, and at a level he couldn't have found otherwise. Total immersion all right! The rogue!"

I try to distract her with some peculiar news. Sue, a colleague of hers that I met during a visit to her lab, rang me a few days ago, asking to meet me. In a coffee shop quite distant from the Company, she told me that the original two embryos had disappeared from the liquid nitrogen canister #9. She knew they were in there because Professor Vladov had asked her not to touch that particular canister. She then went and asked him if he knew where they were. He denied any knowledge.

"Eve, did you know that Tim noted the embryos' storage codes when you disclosed them to Leo at the airport? What do you think happened?"

Eve takes a while to answer. "I can think of only two possibilities. It was either Leo or Tim. Leo to move them to another site for security purposes, in view of future, perhaps secret, implantations; Tim to extract further stem cells and produce more material for the regeneration of organs. I'm sorry, I can't find out more from here."

A week later she sends me a full report on the embryos' testing. It's a very well constructed report which uncovers an impeccably rational method, or as they say, *la mèthode francaise.* It makes clear all the avenues explored, all the possible outcomes, and ends with an interesting, quite definitive conclusion:

"Both embryos are genetically normal but their anomalous growth is due to a unique epigenetic effect. Certain genes, two that are involved in growth control, are abnormally demethylated, lacking therefore the brakes in the dividing cell cycle. Without the inhibition of methyl groups on these two genes, their cells continue to divide, causing an accelerated growth.

"This is the first time such an event has been observed, therefore we can only speculate on how and when the demethylation occurred, whether *in utero* in the embryos or in their parents' reproductive cells."

Well, then, they have excluded genetic abnormalities. Because the epigenetic defect can be corrected, there is now a good chance that the Company will obtain permission to implant the embryos, if they can be found.

Eve hasn't sent any comment to the report. I try for a week to contact her: no luck. She doesn't answer the phone, doesn't send messages. Her parents haven't heard. We are all quite concerned.

Eventually I get hold of Luc, who tells me that Eve is on a week holiday in Normandy on some sort of pilgrimage to St. Thèrèse de Lisieux. This religious fervor is new to her parents and to me. Our worries increase.

Carol plans to go to France, while I keep trying to extract more information from Luc. Has Eve finished her work?

"Yes," he says.

Has she booked her flight back to Australia?

"I don't know, she hasn't mentioned it, but left her stuff in the lab."

What happens now with the embryos?

"Eve said she has a new method for long-term storage and will apply it to them when she comes back from Lisieux."

Then one day I get a cryptic message from Eve: go to my parents' place this evening.

I dine with Carol and Mark. Carol has managed to juggle her many commitments and will leave in a couple of days. We eat in the family room where Carol keeps her laptop constantly on with the email connected. A sharp ring signals an inbound message.

She runs to it and shouts, "It's Eve. She's left a message for all three of us!

"Dearest mother, father, best friend. Don't worry, I am OK, or will be soon. I have been away to sort this out and believe that I've found a solution. You know, what's been hard for me to accept is normality; I mean an uneventful life. The fast embryos changed that, but only fleetingly, and soon I'll have to leave them.

"I thought hard about it and now I've found a way so that I'll be forever connected with their history. You see, if they are stored away for posterity, if they can be preserved in a museum—say the Quai Branly's Museum where ancient human species are preserved—if these two embryos can be considered the very primitive examples of a new human species, even in their undeveloped form, at their very beginning; if I can manage all that, then my name will be linked to them in history. I will be the only ARCHEOLOGIST OF THE FUTURE!

"Now I am asking the three of you a favor. Connect with me on a video link tomorrow morning at 7 AM Sydney time. I want you to witness my solution and record it. Please be there. I love you."

Carol's face is wet with tears, Mark goes outside on the porch and I can't move. Something really strange is happening to Eve, that's clear to the three of us, even if we can't discuss it. Her mental state, her cold approach, her conclusion, all point to red danger.

*

It's the 25th of February. On the bedside table the clock shows date and time, it's 6 am. In an hour we'll know. The morning routine resolves fast enough;. Mark lends me a fresh shirt. I am careful not to cut myself while using his shaving blades. Carol's hands tremble as she prepares breakfast.

And it's soon 7 o'clock.

The connection is easy. We find Eve sitting on a stool in the lab, her hair flowing freely, Australian way. Her lab coat is elegantly cut, without a collar, very feminine. She is wearing lab glasses, large clear plastic to protect her eyes, slightly colored in violet, which gives her the look of an alchemist.

She smiles at us but doesn't speak and moves very slowly. She has a Petri dish in front of her and performs a number of preparatory steps. While at the beginning we couldn't see anything solid in the dish, she now places it under the microscope with camera attached and we see on screen two blastocysts, two blobs of cells, one next to the other.

She adds a drop of a liquid, colored green, and they absorb it, becoming fluorescent. Eve turns the microscope dials to a greater magnification and we see the green embryos as two balls containing grape-like cells gathered on one side, bathing in fluid, plus a string of cells all around that in a circle.

Then she adds a resinous drop on each, a second one, a third, and more until it reaches the size of a large bead. The resin, transparent, the color of amber, agglutinates around the green embryos and solidifies quickly.

Eve takes the dish off the microscope's platform, decants all superfluous fluid and places the bead, solid amber with two green inclusions, in a dark red velvet-lined box with a transparent lid. The box has a metal plaque at the front with the words:

HOMO SAPIENS RAPIDUS.

She takes her glasses off, smiles again and disconnects permanently.

The family room is plunged into silence until a muffled sound breaks out: Carol cries uncontrollably, her thin shoulders shaking, alone, while Mark, slumped in his chair, shakes his head and murmurs, "What has she done? What has she done?" Elbow on the armchair, he puts his hand on the forehead and closes his eyes.

I look at them, parted in their grief over Eve, and can't move.

***

Thirteen

9 June 2017. It's the day of the final verdict for Eve in the Court at Creteil. My train from Paris stops frequently, either at small suburban stations or in-between to let another train change tracks in the opposite direction. There is time, undisturbed, to reflect on these past crazy three years.

My memories here seem to be in a state of dissociation, stored away in separate chapters. Each is retrievable in a way that seems unrelated to the other. Each of them is discrete, as if to spare me cumulative pain.

Eve's Mental Illness

A few days after Eve trapped the embryos in artificial amber, her mother, Carol, arrived in Paris, determined to find Eve and take her back home. Luc, who responded to my plea for help, was there to meet her and to give her news of Eve. She had been admitted to the Paul Guiraud Psychiatric Hospital, near the Villejuif complex where she had been working in the previous five weeks.

The medical staff told Carol that Eve was completely withdrawn (she wouldn't talk or respond in any visible way) and advised her to be patient and discreet. As she told us later, Carol entered Eve's room determined to take charge, walking briskly and sporting a smile.

Eve lay on her bed, her small frame barely visible under white blankets, her brown hair longer and spread on the pillow in a shape, flat and regular like rays, that showed she had remained in the same position for some time.

Eve's eyes were closed and when Carol put a hand on hers, she didn't react. Carol went closer and whispered in her ear a few affectionate words. Eve didn't respond. Carol caressed her and started talking of how much the three of us had worried about her. She talked for a long time, describing the evening we had spent reading her message and preparing for next morning's video link. Wisely, she didn't talk about the entrapment of the embryos.

With the medical staff, Carol maintained a hard-nosed, professional demeanor and made sure they understood her intention to take Eve back to Australia.

They were polite but firm: "*Pas possible.*"

Why wasn't it possible? Carol didn't see any serious medical reason that held Eve in the hospital bed, without any particular treatment, just lying down there with a feeding drip. Slowly, patiently, Carol started feeding her by mouth. Eve at first resisted, then drank a little, then slowly began eating again, and after thirty days, the drip was taken away.

Carol went to see *Le Chef de Service*, the man in charge, and asked if Eve could now be discharged.

"*Non,*" he replied. He also suggested that she talked with the Director of the lab where Eve had been working, and offered to organize an appointment.

Two days later, *Madame le Directeur* received Carol in her office, a small room with an imposing desk, a 19th Century mahogany piece with shaped legs and a semicircular top, the almost straight side turned towards her.

"Madam," Carol said firmly, "how do you explain the apparent order to keep my daughter in hospital?"

"*Chère Madame*, there is no strict obligation for her to stay in hospital. You can take her to a hotel. What she must not do, and I can assure you she'll be prevented from doing, is to leave France."

Carol was astonished, angry and surprised, unable to proffer another obvious question.

But *Le Directeur* continued: "*Mademoiselle* is going to be, how do you say it in English, '*mise en examen*'. It's a judicial term meaning that they are going to investigate the facts to find out if she has indeed committed a crime."

"How?"

"Your daughter has destroyed French property, and living human property *en plus*, which our lab purchased from her Company on the 22nd of January."

Carol thought of a misunderstanding. Surely it was. But her mind went back mercifully to another point the director had made. She could take Eve out of the hospital to her hotel. That's what happened in the afternoon of the same day.

In Sydney, I spent much time with Eve's father, Mark, to comfort him and to be ready for the news he received from Carol. Her messages were, in fact, directed to both, starting a three-person correspondence that kept us closer than ever.

We decided that Eve's mental health should be our first priority and that Carol should find a nice place to live in Paris. It went without saying that the judicial procedure would take, at best, six months.

Through estate agencies I knew in the VI Arrondissement, and with substantial fees payment, Carol found an apartment near the *Jardins du Luxembourg* where she could take Eve for walks and fresh air.

The three of us devised a strategy in three parts: the first one was to record what happened before Eve's dramatic gesture. Each of us had talked with Eve in confidence but we didn't know if the versions were similar: whether her mind was changing at different times; whether she shared different thoughts with each of us.

The second part was to obtain a diagnosis. Our documentation would be sent to David, the psychiatrist in Boston who had seen Eve often the year before, when she was there with Carol. David would suggest the procedure to reach a definitive diagnosis.

I anticipated that David would identify the broad spectrum of conditions Eve might have, but would be unable, without scanning her brain, to come up with a firm conclusion. So I was certain that Eve had to undergo several diagnostic tests. Once we had obtained the definitive diagnosis, we could think of treatment, the third part of our strategy.

We obviously had gone many times over our recollection of what Eve had told us and it didn't take long to put down all the facts. In five days, working all hours, we put together a reasonable document that Carol took care to send to David.

While waiting for David's opinion, Carol and Eve settled down well in the Paris apartment, often taking lunch in one of the open-air restaurants of the Luxemburg Gardens, then going for a walk. Carol talked as much as she could.

Eve was still not talking, nor showing any reaction to what Carol said, but she ate, slept and washed normally. It was a time of great intimacy between them, as Eve, almost twenty-eight, went back to being as dependent as a child.

David's opinion came on the tenth day in an email addressed to all three:

First I should say that you gave me a good document, one that made my task easier. I have considered all your facts, plus those that I was able to observe when I saw Eve here in Boston. At the time I suggested to Carol that Eve presented all the signs of anxiety/depression syndrome. Your testimonies confirmed that, but unfortunately the most recent facts indicate that she has progressed to the paralysis phase.

Anxiety-depression-paralysis can be present in the same individual and expressed at different stages. I can easily detect anxiety symptoms in the early phase" when Eve first disclosed her embryo finding; when she talked with her father about the possibility of great abnormalities in the embryos; and when she was here in Boston talking with me and feeling the distance between her and the embryos.

The depression phase is evident in the messages she sent from Paris to all three of you. Her depression dropped to a new low when she realized that Luc, her great love, would not go to Australia, as she had hoped, but leave for America.

The paralysis phase is one you know about, her current major problem. Usually this change intervenes when the patient feels total despair and can't face her situation. So she turns off, totally overwhelmed. The term paralysis, of course, refers only to the executive function of the brain being in a state of blockage and not to a physical paralysis where, for instance, the spinal cord has been damaged.

I am reasonably certain that Eve has an anxiety-depression-paralysis problem, but I recommend that she undergo a number of brain imaging scans that may or may not confirm my opinion. There are great methods nowadays and I know that the Hospital Paul Guiraud in Paris is very well equipped to deliver this kind of certainty."

All very clear to everyone, but Carol had a problem and sent me a personal message describing it:

I won't admit it to Mark, otherwise he'll worry about me too, but I think I'm exhausted and can barely function for the ordinary care of Eve. I don't think I'll be able to organize the tests she has to undergo. I find the French difficult to understand even when they speak English. Too bad that I spent years in Bern rather than in Geneva!"

It was an obvious call for help. I approached my editor the next day.

"Are you interested in an article on certain adult stem cells, called mesenchymal cells, taken from the bone marrow and described in a study just published by the Gustave Roussy Institute near Paris? Or in the techniques of transplantation of hands and face that French surgeons have perfected?"

"OK, you want to go back there. I get it."

"Or, if you prefer, I could go on leave without pay."

"Nah, you seem to write better when you think in French."

Mark was relieved that I would go. He said he had been thinking of going himself, but feared he wouldn't be of much help. He gave me things Carol had asked for, in fact a case full of them. And thanked me.

Airport, planes, stopover, and I was in Paris again. It was agreed that I wouldn't see Eve, who was settling down well in their apartment, because I was too strongly associated with the embryos. But within 48 hours I was able to talk with a psychiatrist who was once a neurologist and whom I had met a few times at international conferences.

He recalled for me the basis of current neurological tests. Functional magnetic resonance imaging (fMRI) measures blood oxygen levels in various zones of the brain, so it detects areas of neuronal activity during a particular test. Both anxiety and depression, and of course paralysis, leave a particular pattern in this type of scanning.

In patients suffering from anxiety, for example, this scan can detect abnormal levels of activity in the limbic system, the part of the brain that processes emotions. In cases of depression, patients show decreased connection between certain areas of the Default Mode Network (DMN) and the limbic system.

The DMN, he explained, was until recently considered background neuronal noise. Amusingly, it was considered analogous to the Dark Matter in astronomy and to Junk DNA in genetics. All three are by far the largest components in their fields, but of uncertain, even obscure significance.

In fact the Default Mode Network represents a very large set of firing neurons, active all the time, in a perpetual activity that doesn't stop even during anesthesia. Well, this activity can be measured and shown to be altered in several mental illnesses, like depression and paralysis.

"So," he said, "I suggest we take a look at all this stuff."

In and out of the scanning machines, Eve underwent a full battery of tests over several days, and I must say with remarkable patience. At last, David's diagnosis was confirmed; it was a combination of anxiety, depression and paralysis. Carol and I, with Mark on the phone, didn't know whether to be glad or something else.

But the French psychiatrist to whom we now decided to entrust Eve's care said that a clear diagnosis was better for therapy. David, who knew the Frenchman's reputation and trusted him, was to remain an external consultant in the case.

Therapy, all agreed, was going to be a long affair. It would have to include several methods, some with short-term effects, others more protracted but with long-lasting results.

Eve started taking some antidepressant medication known to increase the number of stem cells that become new neurons in the hippocampus. Then there was the possibility of using Transcranial Magnetic Stimulation, a high frequency and repetitive process, which can activate neurons that in some depressions are partially turned off. This method was considered and agreed on, but only for when Eve was ready to have a relatively involved intervention.

Other possible methods included certain psychotherapies, but for some, Eve had to resume communication before she could benefit from them.

The psychiatrist mentioned other ways to trick Eve's mind back to normal.

There was an imagination technique we could try, he said. It was about a 'mental practice' that could induce physical changes in the patient. The brain has much plasticity and changes under many circumstances, even those just imagined.

He persuaded me that I could, unseen, participate in these types of sessions where Eve, in a nearby room in the dark, would summon up certain images at my command. He explained why he wanted me to do it: my voice was familiar to her, I knew her well and could evoke images of a happy past.

"I know," he said, "that you and Eve had a strong intellectual mateship, but stay away from that. It would be too strenuous for her to be engaged in that sort of thinking. Stick to basic emotions, simple things that she liked, and work on them over and over."

And so it was that I spent many hours with Eve, unknown to her, or perhaps recognized; she never gave any hint of it. But with an EEG cap that measured her brain activity, I could see on a screen her reaction to my words, her recognition of certain images I was asking her to imagine and her lack of response to others she was obviously suppressing.

She recognized the names of her parents' dogs, Bell and Nell, and at that point the graphic needle traced on the paper higher peaks, which showed the expansive firing of her brain cells as detected by the EEG sensors.

When this happened, the psychiatrist asked me to repeat the words many times to reinforce the positive effect of her response. It was a long process that I continued until she was too tired to respond.

"Eve," I said another time, "do you remember Lord Howe Island?"

The graph on paper remained flat, so I continued:

"It's where you climbed a bit of Mount Gower. Remember, the mountain from where you looked down on the lagoon? You beat everyone else to that point, even Max."

The graph raised its spikes several times, but when I mentioned Max, it flattened suddenly.

"Don't you remember Max?" I asked, surprised. The needle hardly moved and the psychiatrist signaled a pause. As a nurse took care of Eve, he pushed me into his office.

"Who is Max?"

"My son. They grew up as close friends."

"How close?"

"I don't know if they ever slept together. It's possible."

"If that's the case, Eve might have transferred her rejection of Luc to an earlier memory of an affair with your son. Let's stay away from potential conflicts like this. Let's keep it simple."

"We've never 'done' simple, Eve and me," I said.

"Well, you'd better start now if you want her to improve."

And so, uncannily, I tried over and over to direct her imagination towards a simpler world, pushing her out from the complex, deep tracks she had dug in her brain, sometimes with my very help.

After many sessions of this kind, the psychiatrist thought we should 'read her mind'. He said we could show her certain words on a screen while she was inside the imaging scanner and see which one she particularly reacted to by firing her neurons in certain areas of the brain. It was also a test to find out if she could still read.

"As you know, when neurons fire," he said, "we'll see the image of her brain changing color in certain areas. That activity will tell us that she is reading and responding to the words you'll type."

In the control room, next to the one in which the cold magnetic resonance machine operated, I selected and typed words that had some message for us, words that she might want to tell us.

I started with the word 'Hello' and the visual area of her brain turned mildly yellow. I continued by typing 'I can read' and the same area intensified. More confident, I pressed on with 'I am better' and more than one area of her brain flashed.

We went on for a long while, her reaction to words clearly showing that she could read and was willing to communicate.

But she treated some words with indifference and that resulted in little firing. To others she reacted with greater excitation. In the end, she became unresponsive, even to words she had recognized before. I typed 'Tired?' and she gave a faint response. I typed 'Want to go?' and her response increased. I then wrote in larger letters, 'SLEEP' and her brain image caught fire.

I typed quickly,

'WELL DONE EVE
BACK HOME NOW'.

*

French Court Case

The intricacies of the Napoleonic law, changed and rewritten only in part over the past two hundred years, are formidable. The last attempt, by President Sarkozy, to do away with le *Juge d'Instruction,* the investigative judge, failed for one good reason; it is the last bastion of an independent judiciary in the investigative phase. The rest (*Le Parquet*) is under the control of the Justice Department, therefore the political power of the day.

But my encounters with the independent judge, who had to decide whether to put Eve on trial, did not leave me with a lasting sense of justice. He needed to establish if Eve had damaged her own property or that of the French lab. In other words, he had to decide whether the French lab actually owned the embryos that were later damaged by Eve.

He interrogated me several times, as well as Carol and Mark, but he insisted most on my evidence because I had co-signed the agreement for 'sale' of the embryos to the French lab. What's more, I had conducted the negotiations for the 'sale' from Santo and I had all the copies of our email exchanges.

To me, this correspondence clearly indicated that the 'sale' was an administrative construct and a convenient arrangement that had nothing to do with a proper purchase of the embryos by the French party. Our lawyer, *Maitre* Dubois, thought this was our strongest point.

However, there was also the recording of the ceremony, where it seemed clear that the embryos had been officially transferred to the French, as witnessed and signed by both Eve and me on the 22nd of January.

And unfortunately, on the lab's back-up memory system there was also the recording of the infamous procedure that Eve used to entrap the embryos. On our side there was the Santo correspondence, showing their devious manoeuvres, while on their side there was the crystal clear image of signing the embryo transfer in Paris. The investigative judge opted for France and remanded Eve for trial.

This investigation had already taken more than six months, and the end of the year 2013 was approaching. Carol had taken extended leave from work and was supervising her research lab and PhD students on line to Sydney. Mark decided to move to Paris himself, advised by *Maitre* Dubois that the administration of justice was a long process in France. Luckily, Mark's employer, the Biotech Investment Fund, asked him to work from Paris to learn about opportunities in France and possibly suggest some joint ventures.

Eve was formally charged on the 2nd of December, but given her mental state, she was dispensed from attending court and spent long periods in rehabilitation. Still unseen, I went to see her a few times while she was in the psychiatric labs so that she could hear my voice for comfort. We didn't tell her about the charge for her alleged crime.

In the next two years—mostly in Sydney to write my book on a biotechnology crime—I spent little time in Paris, going there only when necessary, but following up closely the slow movements of the judicial process.

The previous legal investigation had virtually completed the discovery phase, but it seemed that a second, much more minutely forensic procedure, would revisit most facts and testimony, all correspondence and all evidence. Despite the French being very advanced in electronic matters (their communication tool, *Minitel*, was the first ever electronic link between people and organizations), it took more than two years for the case to reach Court.

The administrative tribunal of Creteil was deemed the appropriate jurisdiction: after all, the 'crime' had been committed in nearby Villejuif in a government laboratory. Several audiences took place in the space of two weeks and they called me again to testify in front of the judge.

An extremely polite man, swamped by heavy attire and sweating, he asked me to answer the prosecutor's questions with *franchise* and respect, but without fear; I was not accused of any wrongdoing.

The questioning was, of course, in legal French, a highly sophisticated but very convoluted language that I simplified straight away in my mind, getting to the essential points only. And this is what I'm reporting here.

"*Monsieur,*" the prosecutor started, "you are Australian and perhaps your ancestors were used to the legal/penal system?"

"I am indeed Australian, *Maitre*, but my ancestors were more exactly Italians from a region of Italy invaded by the Bourbons, so it's possible that you and I have common ancestry."

"It is a fact," he continued after a pause, "that you were involved in a devious manoeuvre to conceal the sale of the two embryos to the French laboratory."

"No more devious, I think, than the administrative acrobatics of that laboratory," I interjected quickly to prevent him pushing this point. It worked.

"Was it Dr Latimar's idea to bring the embryos to France?" he asked.

"No, it was the geneticist at Villejuif who requested the embryos' twins. Eve thought that this wasn't necessary for the genetic tests and imagined that the French laboratory could have done with cells extracted from the embryos. But they didn't trust our technology and our ability to extract cells without destroying the embryos. Eve wasn't able to convince them in this sense. They demanded to do the procedure themselves with the intact embryos here."

"Are you implying that they had an ulterior motive in wanting to get hold of the embryos?" he asked.

"I am not here to speculate, *Maitre,* or to respond to your speculations."

"Did you suspend your judgment, your doubts and your imagination when confronted with the choice of signing what you described as an invalid document of sale?" He tended the trap.

"I was merely a friend and an interpreter to her, and I knew that Eve was very keen to have the embryos genetically tested. Everyone, in fact, in Australia and here, was very keen to know the results of the tests. So keen, really, that certain procedures, like the signing of the sale documents, seemed trivial in the context of such an extraordinary phenomenon as that of the mutant embryos."

"Then," the prosecutor said, "you are confirming that the agreement of the sale was indeed entered into knowingly and willingly. Well, that is all, your Honor. I have concluded my questioning of the Australian witness."

I was done. Since Carol and Mark, as parents, had accepted that they could not testify, I was in fact the only Australian witness in Court. I looked at our barrister, *Maitre* Dubois, expecting his cross-examination, but he didn't budge from his seat and looked at me reassuringly.

In the days that followed, with Carol and Mark, I attended as many audiences as I could, while Eve was in psychotherapy, unaware.

Finally today, the 9th of June 2016, the judge will pronounce his verdict after listening to the closing remarks of the prosecutor and the defense barrister. I arrive at the Court building a bit late and sit a few rows behind Carol and Mark, who have their barrister, *Maitre* Dubois, between them. They smile at me: tense little smiles.

The prosecutor launches into a long argument that meanders around with outrage at having French property destroyed; disappointment at the lost opportunity of a glorious result had the embryos been alive and capable of developing into exceptional individuals; and finally consternation at the dismal 'murder of prospective humans'.

It's a stereotypical speech that doesn't impress me.

Next, it's the turn of the defense to embark on a *contradictoire*, the counter argument. *Maitre* Dubois rises and shows us why he was recommended as our barrister. His speech uses language formidable and nuanced that has impact, strength and subtlety. Here I can only sum it up.

"Who owns them?" he asks. "How can you so easily conclude that the property of these embryos has been settled with a one page document, signed by a person who had clearly lost her mental balance and by her friend/interpreter?

"If we go back to the very origin of these embryos, one might possibly argue that in fact the accused had property rights over them, since it was she who created the embryos in her laboratory. It is clear that she was convinced about her rights over them but, after all, she had lost her mind.

"Of course the stronger argument is that the embryos' parents, as the biological originators of the new lives, owned them all along. They consented to their embryos' twins being transferred to France, but only to be genetically tested in order to find out if they carried major abnormalities.

"The laboratory at Villejuif—an excellent facility, one of the best in the world, I must say—did in fact find out that no such abnormalities were present, paving the way for their potential implantation. This was a real possibility, especially since the original two embryos seem to have disappeared in Sydney.

"Against this tragic circumstance—with the parents first rejoicing for the genetic health of their embryos, then realizing that they had been permanently trapped in amber—here comes an administrative claim that not only has no heart, it has no rational basis whatsoever. The very fact that they tried to acquire other people's embryos without their consent indicates dubious ethical standards that cannot be rewarded with a win in this case."

Clearly stung, the presiding judge takes a surprisingly short time to reflect and speaks very quickly, almost in a hurry. "The paralysis of the accused is punishment enough." Then he delivers his verdict, which in English would sound ambiguous: *"Responsable mais pas coupable."*

The operative word here is Not Guilty; Eve is free to go.

Excited, I see Carol and Mark hugging each other, the lawyer, then each other again, with small cries of laughter and tears mixing on their faces. I walk towards them but they don't seem to pay any attention to me, just a passing smile, while M. Dubois asks Carol, "Are you sure you can take Eve home straight away?"

"Yes, I'm hoping tomorrow. She'll be okay, the doctors say, as long as she does more rehab down there. And you? Any chance of your coming to Sydney? You'd enjoy a visit, for sure, and we'd love to see you again. You've done wonders for us."

They shake hands forcefully and then Carol moves towards the door, Mark on her heels. As I watch them leaving, Mark turns back and waves at me, then moves his hands outwards in a friendly gesture that tells me he can't do anything else. I understand.

Epilogue

In my case, going back home straight away was not an option I could consider after Paris. I needed fresh inspiration on how to pay my dues for the debacle and found it in a distant time, in II Century Rome.

After weeks roaming ancient walls, layers of civilizations built one on top of the other, Roman palaces exposed while digging for another metro line, ruins left untouched and monuments restored, I am now inside the *Musei Capitolini* in front of the equestrian statue of Emperor Marcus Aurelius.

Natural light from glass walls to the right and the back of the statue creates a tri-dimensional chiaroscuro of great effect. The power of the statue comes not from an imperious posture, nor from its remarkable size. It is the reach the Emperor's gesture projects, his right hand thrust not in command, but in gentle salute.

Modest self-reliance, a busy life of duty, his *'Meditations'* tell the thoughts of a sincere man who valued nature and knew that there are things in our power and things that are not, who tried to know himself with severity, not self-contempt. A man with power, not arrogance.

That's where we failed, where Eve went mostly wrong with my initial help. In our case, it was scientific arrogance that led us to go about owning nature in one of its exceptions. Now that Eve has paid her price, what is mine?

I think of the possibility of chasing the original embryos; of using my investigative, scientific journalism to find out what happened to them; to write again about their story and, exclusively, about their end. Would Marcus, the man, choose to do that? Or would he want nature to follow its course, allowing the embryos to grow, or die undisturbed, out of the public glare? This is a price I can pay and I'm willing to pay.

I bow to Marcus Aurelius and turn to walk away, sensing a little relief at last. Once outside, I take the Imperial Avenue leading to the Colosseum and start on a reflective stroll under the pale sun of mid-March.

The move—to leave the embryos alone—eases my visceral grip on their story. Slowly my memories take on a new, cooler quality and become more distinct. Now, hovering on them, two words in particular resonate and come repeatedly to the fore: scientific arrogance.

That element eased itself into my relationship with Eve and introduced in our scientific philosophy a belief that kept us apart from good, mainstream scientists like Carol: we know before you know, without proof, because our intellect can jump ahead of yours. Then Eve jumped ahead of me, too far.

What happens now that our company is broken? I search my feelings beyond the memories and think of the present. Entering a space in my mind that seems void and virgin, I hesitate a little and wait until something timidly appears: it is a feeling that is hard to define—not new, perhaps forgotten—but I sense that my present is finally free.

***

Acknowledgments

I wish to thank the people who helped me in this enterprise: Carolyn Adams from Bookish; Rosie Scott from the University of Technology, Sydney; Trevor Shearston and Tom Flood from Flood Manuscripts; Fran Bigman from The Literary Consultancy—London, and Delia Rothnie-Jones from Mosman College for their expert advice. John O'Connor for his exceptional support. Maria Teresa Hooke, Paolo Totaro, Chiara Barbi, Angiolino Logi, Julia Pucci and Marie-Laure Aymonier-Newman for kind suggestions and comments. My son Federico for his fine critique and his sons James and Leo Pucci for fond encouragent. Finally, I thank Lorraine Goldman from Author House for her unflappable cooperation.

Biography

Alessandra A. (Alex) Pucci has been a scientist for more than thirty-five years. After taking science degrees from the Italian Universities of Pisa and Florence, she obtained a Ph.D. in Immunology from the University of Sydney; Alex has written scientific articles while working in medical research. Later, she took up courses in journalism and published scientific articles for the general public in several journals.

Alex is based in Sydney, Australia, but has also lived elsewhere: in Eritrea (Africa) where she was born from Italian parents; In Italy, in Pisa and Florence; in France, in Nice and Paris. Alex also spent several months in the USA as 1987 Eisenhower Fellow (Multination Program).

In Australia, Alex founded two Biotech companies in 1981 and 1996.

Over two decades in Australia, Alex has been appointed to various Government advisory roles, including membership of the Science and Technology Council that advises the Prime Minister and Cabinet. She was made an Officer of the Italian Republic and an Officer of the Order of Australia. She was also awarded the Centenary Medal, all for services to Science and Industry. Her story is recorded in the National Library of Australia and in the book 'Profiles': Australian Women Scientists by Ragbir Bhathal. Alex is a Fellow of the Australian Academy of Technological Sciences and Engineering.

The artist:
Janet Laurence, a prominent Australian artist, is at www.janetlaurence. com

Credits

Images courtesy of artist Janet Laurence and ARC ONE Gallery, Melbourne.

Author photo—Sally Coffey